# ANNIE

For Sue

Bought in Phillipsburg,

Love
Myra

August 12, 2014

Tiana

This book is dedicated to my sister, Ellen, who encourages my writing of Montana based historical novels.

# ANNIE

## The Cabin In The Woods

A TRUE STORY

From slavery
To A
Montana Homestead.

Philipsburg, Montana Territory.

1833 – 1914

## Lenore McKelvey Puhek

iUniverse, Inc.
New York   Bloomington

# TABLE OF CONTENTS

▼

Annie Morgan's tombstone, Philipsburg Cemetery

# Introduction

A letter to my readers:

This novel wanders a bit from my usual historical accounts. Last summer, while walking around in the old cemetery at Philipsburg, Montana, looking for...I didn't know what...a rather unusual stone, obelisk shaped, white, with a cross on top, caught my attention. It stood higher than other stones, defying the wind to erase its inscription.

Curiosity leads me to stand in front of it. *Mrs. Agnes "Annie" Morgan 1914*, reached out to me. The backside of the tombstone revealed almost unreadable words: *cooked for General George A.Custer, a good neighbor and liked by all who knew her.*

Something clicked within me. I wanted to write about this unique Montana pioneer woman.

Research drew me deeper into her life story of 81 years. I discovered that she had a companion in Joseph (Jocko, a.k.a. Fisher Jack) Case, (1846-1930) buried near Annie.

His story is the life of 84 years of adventure: as a trapper, miner, Civil War Union soldier, Indian fighter, and drifter; whose passions in life were driving automobiles and fishing Rock Creek near Philipsburg, Montana.

As his death neared, he wrote his final wishes from his bed at the Old Soldiers Home in Columbia Falls, Montana. One very important wish, written in pencil, stated, *Don't send me back east for burial, but take me to the Philipsburg Cemetery to be buried near my Annie.*

They lived a common-law marriage. It was against the laws of the State of Montana for an inter-racial couple to marry until 1953. Together they worked on a jointly owned homestead near the Hog Back on Rock Creek, in Montana territory.

Collectively, much of our colorful Montana history passed between them. They celebrated Montana's entrance into Statehood. Jocko voted for the first time. Annie, being female, was not allowed to vote.

Further searching lead me to old-time residents of Philipsburg. They shared wonderful stories about Annie and Jocko. They escorted me to see the homestead. With all this information, it was time to weave the present with the past.

The sprits of Agnes Annie Morgan and Joseph a.k.a. Jocko a.k.a. Fisher Jack Case, will always hover over their Rock Creek homestead, whether I write their story or not. However, in Part Two it is my desire to bring this couple's illustrious past into the present day contemporary lives of my readers, imagining that the loop of life continues beyond our understanding or our reasoning.

Happy reading,

Lenore McKelvey Puhek

April 6, 2009

▼

# Spring 1880

"Whoa! There, horse."

Her dog, Bingo, had set up such a barking frenzy that Annie threw open her front cabin door. She saw a riderless horse come prancing into her yard. She cautiously approached the skittish animal, hoping to grab the reins that flipped up in the tall grass with every step the horse took. The gelding sidestepped towards her, swinging his head and mane. Annie reached out, and with her left hand, was able to grab a stirrup. Then she caught hold of the reins.

"Whoa! There, fella. You're okay."

Calmly, Annie talked down the agitated animal. "How come you're riderless?" She led the large, black horse over to her hitching post and tied the reins.

"What you doin' out here without your mastah?" The animal swung his hindquarters in a half circle, stamping his hooves into the soft mountain meadow grasses that grew all around the cabin.

"Let me have a look at you. I don't see anything broken, or bleedin', and the saddle cinch is tight, so what happened out there?" She slowly looked around the yard, noticing that darkness would soon fall. "A mountain lion scare you away from camp?"

Then Annie realized that the reins were wet. The horse must have been in the river.

"Where did you buck off your mastah? Can you tell me?" The horse started to whinny as if trying to talk to Annie.

Bingo had been barking and jumping around. But now, as if listening to a sound Annie could not hear, Bingo stopped whining. He turned to face the fast flowing water. The dog headed toward the river's edge, whirling around trying to get Annie to follow.

"Slow down, Bingo. I'm comin'." Annie was searching along the bank, when she saw a man facedown in the ice-cold mountain stream.

*What the…? He needs help…if he's still alive that is.* Annie splashed into the cold stream, grabbed the man by his collar, and pulled his head up and out of the water. She then turned him over onto his back, and began dragging him over the rocks to the bank.

"Give me strength. Oh Laws! What have I fished out of this old Rock Creek tonight?" Annie, strong and able from her early years as a slave on a large southern plantation, lived alone. She worked her homesteaded land near Philipsburg, Montana Territory.

"I never thought I'd be catching me a man this way," she mumbled to the dog. Bingo was jumping back and forth over the man. He'd sniff the body, then run down the trail, only to retreat back to Annie who struggled to try and carry the man. She finally dropped him back onto the ground.

"Sorry Mistah'. But I just can't do it any other way."

She grabbed his boots in both her hands, and found it easier to drag him back to her cabin.

"Besides, you are out cold and as stiff as a tree log, so's I don't suppose you'd know or care as long as I got you out of the water." She kept up a dialog with the man, even though she knew he was unconscious.

"Who are you, anyway, and what you doin' in my river?" Annie pulled and tugged him back to her cabin. She was able to get the body through the cabin door. She lifted the stranger to her bed, and dropped him onto the mattress.

"Now what do you make of this kettle of fish?"

The man moaned, and Annie took that as a good sign. "I'll get you under them covers and get you warmed up, but first you got to wake up." With a couple of gentle slaps to the man's face, he started to respond.

Annie pulled off his boots, then took off his wet outer Levi pants, his fishing vest and flannel working man's shirt. "Now we goin' to get you out of that long underwear." Annie laughed, realizing she was undressing a stranger in her bed. "It's for your health, suh. I must get you under the sheets, and get you warmed up."

Annie was sweating as she worked to save the man's life. She was soaked from the cold water, too, and knew it was just a matter of time before the chills would take over her body. She kicked off her wet boots, pulled off her cotton dress and shrugged into a flannel nightgown. She found a pair of wool socks and put them on her feet, then added leather slippers before returning to the still delirious man.

She reached for a pan, and filled it with hot water from the teakettle she kept on the back of the wood stove. Then she grabbed a rag and dipped it into the warm water. She returned to the stranger in her bed, and started sponging water onto the man's forehead, cheeks, chin and neck. She rinsed the rag, and returned to her job at hand, working tirelessly over the man's hands, arms, torso, legs, feet. She could feel him stirring at her touch. She watched his face, hoping to see some color return to his skin.

"Ah! Good sign, there Bucko. Let's get you woke up here, so I can get you to drink some of my good herbs. We got to get the insides of you warm too. That river is mighty cold this time of the year, don't you know?"

The man had opened his eyes and had tried to speak, but was too weak. He raised his arm once, but it fell listless by his side, to rest on the bed. Annie folded his arm back under the blankets. She felt his forehead, feeling the burn through her gentle touch.

"Mercy me. I think you're goin' to make it, Mistah. I am Annie Morgan, and I just fished you out of Rock Creek. Another few minutes and you would've been a gonner. What you doin' out this far in the mountains? I like company stoppin' by, but you didn't have to be so dramatic. Most people knock on my cabin door." Annie kept talking, giving herself time to decide what to do with the fellow.

"You got chills, *and* you got a fever, suh. I am going to give you some herbs for that, and we got to get somethin' on your stomach."

Annie moved to her kitchen cupboard and found the ingredients to make an herbal tea. She opened the tin to take out a pinch of leaves.

Iffen you got typhoid fever you'll need this medicine, and, iffen you don't, it won't hurt you to drink it. Yes, I know it stinks. Hold your nose and swallow it." She filled a small cup with the warm liquid, and carried a spoon with her back to the bedside. She sat on a little three-legged stool. She put one hand behind the man's head.

"Now jess let me give you sips, suh. Let it drain down into your throat, and you jess let me do the work of gettin' you well. I do know about nursin' men back to health."

Annie smiled. The stranger in her bed, with glazed eyes searching hers, smiled back. He obeyed his nurse's orders, and was able to take a few sips before collapsing back onto the pillow.

"Will you marry me?" He barely whispered before he passed out again.

Annie smiled as she walked over to the cabin door and opened it for some fresh air. Bingo was still standing guard over the horse tied up to the post.

Still dressed in her flannel nightgown, Annie tossed a hand-woven wool shawl around her shoulders. She kicked off her leather slippers and dropped her feet into a pair of Wellingtons that she wore while working in the garden.

"Come on, Bingo, let's give this critter some food and put him in the barn for the night." The moon was full, and the night air fragrant with the perfume of honeysuckles from the vine that grew up the side of the porch railings. The horse walked easily behind Annie as she led him to the barn.

"Your goin' to be jess fine tonight, horse, so don't be frettin' no more."

Annie removed the saddle and bridle after she put the horse into a stall. She dropped a couple of armloads of hay in with the horse, called to Bingo to come with her, and returned to the cabin.

"I'm back, suh. Your horse is mighty fine. He's confined in my barn, along with your saddle and gear." Annie continued to talk out loud to the stranger in her bed, even though there was no response. She bustled about the room, adding more wood to the stove. She kept one eye on her newly acquired patient, hoping for some movement. She watched his breathing and noted it was steady and deep.

"That's good, Mistah. You jess keep on warmin' up some. I'm goin' to heat you some chicken broth. You know. Every ailment heals with chicken soup." Annie went to her larder and found some of her homemade canned broth, which she opened and poured into a saucepan. The kitchen stove was hot, and the liquid warmed up fast. Again, she carried the bowl of soup to the bedside. Again, she gently slapped his cheeks to wake him up. This time the response was much quicker.

"Welcome to the cabin of Annie Morgan, Mistah. Take a slow sip of this broth. You'll feel better right away." She was able to get a couple of spoonfuls into the man, and was pleased he did not vomit it back at her. She made a mental note to get a bucket to put by his bed. "This is goin' to be a long night," she whispered to Bingo. He had let down his guard stance to lie by the front door.

"Out here in Hog Back Mountain country is a far ways from folks who must know you over in Philipsburg. After wonderin' your name, I'd like to know where you come from." She again slapped her patient on his cheeks. "Mistah, you stay awake for a while now, hear me?" With two fingers pinching his nose back, she opened his mouth to examine his tongue.

"Ah-ha. Jess like I thought. Mistah. I think you's down with the typhoid fever. Your tongue is covered with crud and all dried up, your eyes are glazed, and you're burnin' up. Those red spots on your chest are surefire signs, too. Laws, what am I goin' to do with you?"

Annie smiled down at the very ill man, who had suddenly started shivering again, even under the heavy wool blankets Annie had tossed over him.

"Guess this calls for my doctorin' kit." Annie walked into her tiny closet, searched the shelf until she spotted a black doctor's medical bag, and pulled out a book.

Bingo-drawing of dog

▼

# JOSEPH

The darkness closed down around Annie. The only light, visible from the outside, was a lone lantern glow that continued to burn until near dawn. Annie tended to the ill man as best she knew how. Her well-used and dog-eared medical book advised that if her patient, indeed, had typhoid fever, then sleep was good, once the patient had regained consciousness.

He would need water and liquids to stop dehydration, and Annie read that this sickness could take several weeks to overcome. Also, it was highly contagious, but Annie remembered having had typhoid fever as a young girl. The medical book said a person only caught it once in a lifetime, so Annie was not worried for herself.

Yesterday had been a long, hard workday for Annie in her garden and hay meadow, and she was tired by evening fall. To stay awake the whole night was a struggle for her, but she knew she had to maintain a wakefulness.

She lost count of the hot teas she had made, the chicken broth she had spooned into his throat, and the logs of wood she'd put into the stove. But, with the dawn came a positive sign. The man was awake, the glazed look gone, and he complained of a very dry, sore throat.

"Where am I? And who the heck are you?" asked the stranger stretched out in Annie's bed. He was surprised to see a woman of color frowning down at him.

"Well, for a man who proposed to me not more than twelve hours ago, that is one fine thing to hear this mornin'."

She moved toward the man and put her hand on his forehead. The fever had broken during the night. Annie had continued to bathe his head and shoulders. It pleased her that the heat had not returned. The man appeared stronger. Sometime during the middle of the night, Annie had felt comfortable with his falling asleep, as it was not fitful.

"I think you are the one who needs to tell me some answers, suh."

She sat down in her rocking chair and gently rocked with her right foot. "I fished you out of the river yesterday evening. Your horse is in my barn, fed and watered and in fine shape." Annie continued to rock, back and forth. She was waiting for the man to jump in with answers, but he said nothing.

"Maybe you don't remember nothin'?" She frowned at the thought that he might be suffering from amnesia from the fall into the rocks in the bottom of Rock Creek. Back and forth went the rocking chair.

"Can you give me some water, please? My throat is so dry it hurts to move my tongue, and my back and stomach hurt."

"Sure can, Bucko. But how about a name for me to be callin' you first?" She rose from the chair and went to the wooden bucket that sat on the edge of the counter top. She carefully ladled a few ounces into a Mason jar, used now for a glass since it had a slight chip in the rim, and walked back to the bed.

"I think you have typhoid fever, suh, and if you do, please be careful with how much water you drink. Just a few sips at a time. I don't need you vomitin' all over my cabin."

The sick man stared up at her from the bed, as if he was trying to remember something very important.

"Case. My name is Joseph Case." He smiled at Annie. "Thank you for helping me and my horse."

Bingo stood between Annie and the stranger, not growling, but being sure to let the man know he was in the room guarding his mistress.

"Go lay down, Bingo. He's okay," said Annie. Bingo returned to his guard spot by the door but kept his eyes on the man.

"So, Joseph Case, you from around these parts? I don't remember seein' you. What were you doin' in my mountains yesterday?"

Joseph swung his feet out of the bed and sat up. He pretended to be stronger than he really was, and Annie made note of it.

"Here, now. Don't you go lookin' for your clothes. I got them strung all aroun' the cabin dryin' out. You were drownin' in Rock Creek when Bingo here found you face down in the river. So, jess take it easy, and let me nurse you back to health in a couple of days." She moved to the stove and put fresh warm broth into his bowl but left the spoon on the table.

"Here you go. Try and sip this a little at a time. We got to get some nourishment into your sorry bag o' bones." She wondered what to do about the outhouse, but decided he was too dehydrated at the time to worry about it yet. She would find a pail in the barn when she went out to feed the chickens and milk the cow. She had chores that had to be tended to regardless of how tired she felt. Now, she needed to turn her attention to the man's horse.

"What's your horse's name? I need to go tend to him now. If I put him into my hay field, will he stay aroun' waitin' for you to come back? Or do you want me to hobble him?"

Joseph looked at her with clear eyes. "I asked you to marry me? Well, what was your answer, or did you give me one?" He took a swallow of the broth, and the two stared at each other.

"Please suh, I need some answers from you. I want to get you out of my bed and on your way, but I can't do that without your givin' me some answers."

"Yes, of course," said Joseph. "They know me in the Philipsburg area, but I live in these mountains most the year 'round. I'm a wild game hunter, and I supply meat to the cooks for the pots bubbling around the clock for the miners in Granite County." He stopped and frowned.

"I guess I must have been hunting when I came out this way. A few days ago, I thought I was coming down with something, but just kept on moving this way. Sure glad I did, too. Seeing as how I landed here." He made a sweep with his hand, almost knocking over the glass of water now standing on the three-legged stool. Annie was not impressed.

"I'm goin' to take care of your horse. Don't you move out of that bed. I don't want to come back in here and find you out cold on my kitchen floor. You hear?" She put her hands on her hips. "I repeat. What is your horse's name, and will he stay put?"

"Charlie. My horse's name is Charlie. He won't leave without me on his back."

She reached for her old, faded shawl and put on her well-worn straw hat. "I'll be back in with your gear. I noticed a rifle in a scabbard on your saddle. You might be more comfortable with it here in the house."

The door slammed shut behind her. *My, my…An Irishman with a sense of humor.*

Annie was happy to be outside in the fresh air. She walked with Bingo to the barn and heard the horse stomping around inside.

"Well, Charlie, good mornin' to you. Your mastah is goin' to be jess fine." Annie moved slowly and talked calmly to the spirited animal. "I'm goin' to let you out into my hay meadow, Charlie, and you gotta promise me you'll stick around and not give me or Bingo any trouble."

She filled a wooden bucket full of oats and approached the black horse. She grabbed his mane and stroked his neck before putting a halter over his head and ears. Now she could lead the animal outside without fear of his running away from her.

She enticed Charlie with the bucket of oats and led him into the field. She set the bucket on the ground, near the gate, and walked over to the water pump. Fresh water filled a metal tub and the horse drank long gulps. "Hhmm. I hope you aren't sick too."

Bess and Ben, Annie's team, came over to the new horse and stared at him.

"Well, you two, meet your new room mate." She poured them some oats, also.

"Now, you all get along." Annie took off the halter and gave Charlie a swat on the rump. "Have a lazy day, Charlie. I'll be back to check on you."

Annie returned to the barn. She remembered to pick up a metal basin in case she needed it for Joseph, should he be nauseated from the chicken broth. She also picked up a bucket for him to use for his private needs.

*And people think I live a dull life stuck out here at the foot of Hog Mountain.* Annie hurried back to her cabin, hoping to find everything as she left it. *First thing I gotta do is open some windows and get some fresh air in there.*

"Charlie is up to his knees in the meadow, has fresh water and a bucket of oats. He'll be okay until he sees your ugly mug." Annie noted that Joseph had swallowed all of the chicken broth and the water. Both vessels were empty. "That's good, suh. You're on the road to feelin' better already. I told you last night I was goin' to nurse you back to the livin'."

Both laughed, because when Annie had said it to him last night, she was making conversation and trying to keep herself awake. Case apparently had heard her through his fog. What Annie was really saying was "Iffen I don't get your fever down you are goin' to die in my bed, and then what am I goin' to do with you?"

Bingo

# ~ 3 ~

▼

# ANNIE'S CABIN

Joseph woke in darkness. A strange sound had roused him from a dreamless, yet drifting sleep. A muffled sound... squeak, tap, roll, squeak, tap, roll...assaulted his ears, over and over again, in a steady rhythm.

*Where am I? Where is Charlie and my rifle? Where are my pants?* Joseph looked down at his body and actually gave a sigh. *Looks like I've been ill and somebody is nursing me. Well, I just have to wait and find out I guess. Sure wish I had my rifle beside me though.*

The noise stopped.

"You awake or just fitful?" Annie rose from the rocking chair that she had slept in off and on through the long night. The lamp had gone out, she noticed, but soon the sun would be coming up over the hill and she would not need to refill the lantern until daylight. She walked to the stove, checked the gauge and tossed in another log. *Sure would be nice to have a fireplace at a time like this.*

Joseph lay very still in the bed. "Howdy, Ma'am." He looked around him and made a feeble attempt to make a joke. "Thanks for the lodging. I'm awake now and hungry as an old bear."

Annie jumped at the sound of his voice. "Good mornin', suh. I'm happy to see your eyes open this good day that is jess beginnin'."

"Do you remember our conversation from yesterday?" She doubted he did, but wanted to hear it from him. "You gave me a name for your horse.  Can you tell me what it is?"

Joseph laughed. He instantly took a liking to this woman who was tending to him and to his horse. "His name is Charlie. At least the last time I saw him that's what he was called. You thinking to go trading him off for my medical bill payment?"

"Not hardly, suh." Annie bristled. "I have not left your side for three days. With the help of my dog, Bingo, we fished you out of Rock Creek. He has been watchin' you ever since." Annie put her hand on the man's forehead and was pleased to see he was not hot. His blue eyes were clear. She walked over to her makeshift clothesline and grabbed the man's clothes, socks, and boots. She set them on the edge of the bed.

"You feel up to try walkin' around inside the cabin?"

"Yeah. I'd like that" he said. "By the way, my name is Joseph Case, in case you forgot from yesterday when you asked me about my horse."

Annie laughed. "I like a man with a sense of humor." She walked to the edge of the bed and extended her arm and the man grabbed hold. He put his legs over the edge of the bed and started to stand up, wearing nothing but his birthday suit.

"Suh! Wait! You are naked as the day you were born. Here, put your pants on." She turned away from him, and backhandedly held out his pants. Joseph chuckled at Annie's obvious discomfort, but he slipped into his Levis.

Annie took note of the size of the stranger. He was taller than she realized, and muscular, for being rather slim built. He appeared to be younger than she thought, too. His reddish-colored beard was trimmed, and he had the look about him of a jaunty Irishman.

She didn't notice, but Joseph's eyes had been following her every movement. He shakily buttoned the fly, but felt the effects of three days in bed.

"Hhhmm. I need to sit back down. I'm sorry to be such a bother, ma'am. By the way, I think your name is Annie? How do you do?"

Annie smiled. "You jess set there, Joseph. I'll fetch you some water.  That is all you need right now." Annie hesitated for a moment. She reached up and tugged on her dress collar.

"I have another name for you," said Annie, rather shyly. "Joseph is just too formal of a name for a mountain man. How's about tryin' on Jocko for a name?"

Joseph looked at Annie and saw a woman, sitting with downcast eyes, waiting for his answer.

"That is a perfect name for me, Annie. I like it...Yes, Jocko it is from here on out." He reached for another slice of bacon, and broke the spell they both felt that had come into the cabin.

Annie busied herself cleaning up the breakfast dishes. She told herself that they would meet again, someday in Philipsburg, when she brought in vegetables and eggs from her underground root cellar.

This year, she would have extra jams and cabbages for sale, too. Her garden took up more than an acre of land, and she tended it carefully every day. Her chickens roamed freely in the garden area, and she had a small, inadequate pen for them at night. Come fall she would butcher some of them for sale, and for her own use. Annie canned chickens, and wild game, and vegetables to keep her alive during the long winter months.

Jocko leaned back in his chair. He reached for the sugar bowl and took out some cubes to take out to his horse as soon as he could walk more than a few feet without getting all shaky.

"Annie, I am a meat supplier for the mining camp cooks. I was out this way looking for game, and I was fishing Rock Creek when I was overcome." He stopped talking but then added, "I'll bet they are wondering where I am with their meat for the pots."

Annie nodded. "Well, your fishin' pole is probably way down-river by now, but I'll take a walk downstream from where I found you, and see if it might have been caught in the brush along the creek bed or somethin'. Your creel was wrapped around the horn on your saddle, and your rifle was in the scabbard. I'll fetch your gear inside when I go out to feed the chickens, and when I need to tend your horse again this mornin'." Annie paused. "I also have to go milk Bossie before her calf takes all the milk. I think it's safe to leave you inside the cabin, don't you?"

Annie didn't talk much, except to Bingo, since she lived alone so far back in the mountains and didn't have much company. During the summer, fishermen would camp along the creek. Annie made small talk with them, cooking their catch and making apple pies and cookies for sale. This was a good way for her to bring in a bit of income.

Hardly anyone stopped by during the winter months. On occasion, a neighbor would pass by, but usually the deep snows kept everyone pretty much next to home. Annie had a wagon and a sled pulled by her faithful work team, when and if, she needed to get out.

She didn't mind being *alone,* but sometimes *loneliness* overcame her. She realized she was actually enjoying the stranger's company. *Better not get too friendly, Annie. He'll be gone in a couple of days. Wait and see.*

"Why don't you come sit outside while I make you some breakfast? The sun is up, the wind is down, and I think you'd like some fresh air in your lungs."

Annie took his arm and helped him to the chair on the porch. Then she poured water into the coffee pot, added some grounds, and set it on the stovetop. She decided to make him a weak, soupy oatmeal mixture for his first meal back from the dead. *Jess in case he can't keep it down after all.*

Coffee aromas wafted easily and Joseph heard his stomach growl. He was sitting in a straight-backed chair on the front porch and he really wanted a cup of good strong coffee.

"Ma'am, I'm ready for a cup of coffee, can I come inside yet?" he called out. He used a falsetto voice, "P-l-e-a-s-e?"

*Why does that man make me laugh with everything he says?* Annie thought with a smile.

"Breakfast is ready for you, suh."

Joseph walked through the open kitchen door and sat, grateful for the bowl of watery oatmeal Annie set before him.

"You keep that down, and in about an hour I'll make you a real hearty breakfast. But I have to tend to your horse now. You eat up, now, you hear?"

Annie and Bingo left the cabin and made the short walk to the barn. This morning Charlie was ready for her with a soft nicker.

"You want some oats, do you? Okay. Let's put on the halter and get you to the meadow today." Annie went through the routine of catching the animal.

"Iffen there is time, maybe I'll give you a good brush." She led Charlie outside and over to the main field where the two horses stood alongside the fence.

"You two curious? She released the halter from Charlie and admonished the animals to play together. She was not worried that they would not get along, but sometimes Bess could be mighty standoffish if she thought there was an intrusion into her world...or rather into her field. *I'll keep track of them but so far so good.*

When Annie returned to the cabin she was surprised to find Joseph Case had dressed, eaten his oatmeal, and found his way to the outhouse without any problems. He was slowly working his way back to the cabin when she spotted him.

"Good for you, suh. You are healin' very fast. That is a good thing, and I would think you would be ready to ride on out of here in a few more days. Most patients need at least forty-eight hours to see iffen they're goin' to make it, but you are strong otherwise, I can see." Secretly, she did not want him to leave too soon.

Joseph patted his vest and smiled at Annie.

"I am ready for some eggs, if you have them, Ma'am?"

Annie flinched at the sound of "Ma'am." It made her sound old.

"Eggs comin'right up. I need some breakfast myself. How about some homemade bread and strawberry jam?"

Annie pointed outside to her garden. "I have my own plants in my garden, and between the birds and the rabbits, we all manage to get a few of the berries during the summer months."

They were comfortable during the meal, with Annie asking questions about his hunting skills and he, in turn, interested in how she managed to live all alone on her homestead.

"Come and take a short walk with me. Not too far from my cabin door, now. I can point out the river and where I found you. I think Charlie would like a pat or two from you, too. He might be feelin' a bit confused as to what happened to you."

Annie had dropped the "suh" and "Mistah" from the conversation, and she noticed Joseph had done the same, calling her "Annie" instead of "Ma'am." Annie liked that familiarity.

## ~ 4 ~

▼

# JOSEPH ASKS FOR WORK

Joseph stood up without help, his strength rapidly returning thanks to Annie's tender care. They prepared to leave the cabin together, to walk into the warmth of a late spring day's sunshine.

"Here. You better wear this old hat." She handed him one of her beat up straw hats that hung on hooks by the kitchen door. "Your pale Irish skin will burn outside today, and laws, that beard don't offer you no protection."

She plunked the other hat onto her own head, covering the coarse black hair that hung in a long braid below her shoulders. She chose the path, and led the man to the meadow where he could see his wonderful animal, Charlie.

Watching the horse and Jocko interacting was viewing a bond of love between them. Charlie sensed Jocko's return and, with a wild burst of energy, pranced to the fence, whinnying and tossing his mane. Jocko's whole body grew taller and he seemed stronger as he increased his step. Jocko reached for his faithful horse's head, scratching his forelock, grabbing into his long, flowing mane. Annie felt like an intruder, and she held back so as to not interject her presence.

"Well, you old reprobate. It looks like Annie has been taking mighty good care of you, too. Look at you strutting your stuff in a meadow full of grasses that scrape your belly." Jocko stood there, talking to an old friend. Then, suddenly, he turned and walked back to Annie.

"Okay. Let's take that walk. Charlie's just fine."

Annie pointed out the property line that needed fencing, and then she turned the corner and stopped. "Over there is where I plan to build a new barn. I want one sturdy enough for this country that will stand for a hundred years of winter's snow. It gets over four feet high on the flat back in here most winters."

Jocko walked beside her. *How can this woman accomplish all she has in mind to build? I wonder if…*

"Jocko…you okay? Do you want to stop and rest here on this stump?" Annie motioned toward the large tree stump that dominated the front yard area.

"No, no. I'm fine. What are you planning for over here by the garden?"

Annie smiled. "I'd like a sturdy chicken coop, one with wire fencin' for summer time and shutters for the cooler nights of spring and fall. During the summer, I have a large flock, but I don't keep more than a half-dozen chickens in the winter, wouldn't you know."

"I like fresh eggs in the winter, so I keep back settin' hens and a rooster. Come spring, I get chicks for the next season flock. I keep them in the barn until it gets below zero temperatures. Then they spend nights inside the cabin with me. I have a crate to keep them in, and I toss a blanket over the top of that so they quiet right down. Every small critter that doesn't hibernate, finds its way inside this cabin some time durin' the winter spells."

Annie walked to her garden gate.

"Wild creatures visit my garden during the evenin' hours. As long as they share with each other, I can share with them. But I do need a fence dug down into the ground around parts of the garden, to keep the rabbits from scooting under, and tearing the tops off my carrots." Annie sighed and reached for her hips and straightened her spine.

"There's more here than I can manage. But, it seems I get a lot of dreamin' done durin' the winter. My wish list grows too long by spring."

Jocko listened carefully.

"You ever take on a hired hand?"

"You applyin' for the job?"

"Maybe."

Both stopped talking. Annie closed the garden gate behind her.

"Let's let out my chickens."

She lifted the door latch and the old piece of wood screeched partially open. A flutter of feathers flew past as the birds sprang into the fresh air in search of bugs to eat. Annie reached for a basket hanging on a large hook.

"I'm goin' to collect the eggs."

She left Jocko alone and was happy for the break in the conversation. She needed to return to her daily routine, to be alone, to work the soil in the garden, to check on her animals, to go fishing. Anything to get away from the handsome white man asking too many questions. Questions she had no ready answers for.

Jocko wandered about the yard, making mental notes. An old sawmill stand was set up on the far end of the field. He could set that to running in no time. With all the trees on her property, he could make the lumber needed for that barn of her dreams. He could do a lot of the chores, but would she be able to cope with a man stepping into her space? Would he be able to take orders from this very strong, independent woman?

Annie marched past him with the basket. She kept her pace and disappeared inside the cabin, not to come out again. Only when she heard the sound of wood being chopped did she look out the window.

"Laws, man, are you crazy?" She yelled out into the yard where Jocko had found the axe stuck in the woodpile. The screen door slammed behind her as she ran over to the woodpile.

"Well, Annie, I know you burned up a lot of your wood keeping me warm these past few days, and I want to replenish your supply before I leave."

Annie put her hand to her mouth.

"Are you feelin' up to leavin' already? I think you better come inside. You need a bowl of some hot vegetable soup that's a bubblin' on the stove. A cup of herbal tea and a slice of apple pie will fill you up. Come on in."

Jocko handed over the axe. He hoped that Annie would not notice the beads of sweat on his forehead or the unsteadiness of his gait. He headed for the outhouse.

On the porch, Annie had set out a towel next to the washbasin filled with hot water. Jocko thoroughly scrubbed his hands up to his elbows, splashed warm water on his face and beard, and combed his fingers through his rusty-colored hair.

Annie watched him as he dumped the water onto her lilac bush.

"I have stripped the bed and need to wash the sheets and blankets. I want to get them out into the sunshine where they can dry. You're next on my list to give you a good scrub down, too. We need to clear out the sickness you brought into the cabin."

She laughed, and she saw that he did too. He noticed that the straw mattress had also been taken outside to air in the warmth of the afternoon sun.

"Sit down at the table, Jocko. Don't be holdin' yourself. I can see you are pale, if a white man can ever look paler than he already is." She pulled out a straight-back chair, and he dutifully sat, resting his elbows on the tabletop.

"I think you better rest a bit. We overdid…you bein' out of bed so soon." She reached for his forehead, and saw he was warm and sweating again. Annie poured him some water and handed it to him.

Jocko drank without protest. He trusted Annie's doctoring skills. He made his way to the bed, and dropped himself down full length onto the bare canvas. Annie's bed was made of ropes stretched across the sideboards, and tied in knots. A canvas topped the ropes, and the straw mattress topped it all off.

"Sorry about the mattress airin' outside." Annie tossed a flannel sheet over the top of him, and left him to rest.

Within the hour she had the wash hung out to dry, and was very happy for the sunshine. Bed sheets were not something she had an extra supply of. Annie moved about with an abundance of energy.

*I should be flat on my back needin' sleep. After lunch I'll take a nap in the rockin' chair and leave Jocko to his own self.*

Annie dumped out the wash water into her bushes and vines that grew along the porch railing. She had planted the lilac bushes so long ago she actually forgot what year, but they bloomed and perfumed her yard in late spring. She looked around her homestead with a great sense of pride. She was middle aged, healthy, strong and happy. That was a combination few could claim, and she guarded her health wisely.

If only she had extra money to hire a handyman. *What a treat that would be to finish off projects that have been on my list for years. But that's jess wishful thinkin'.* She'd talk to Jocko as soon as she thought he was sincere in his offer to help out for a few weeks. Maybe a deal could be struck that would benefit them both. *Maybe now is a good time to bring it up,* she decided.

"I have the garden to tend to, cannin', fish to catch and smoke, plus another cuttin' off the meadow for hay for the horses this winter. The days will start growin' shorter here soon, and I don't want to get caught with the first freeze that usually hits around the fifteenth of September." She stopped, thought a minute and then made her offer.

"Jocko, out in the barn I've got a cot stored. You'd be warm out there through the summer and fall months. I can certainly use your hands to get the chicken coop built. And, gettin' the fences done would be a great relief before goin' into winter."

"Then let's shake on it, Annie." Jocko stuck out his rough, calloused hand and shake-on-it they did.

## WARSHING CLOTHES

Build fire in backyard to heat kettle of rain water.
Set tubs so smoke wont blow in eyes if wind is pert.
Shave one hole cake of lie soap in boilin water.

Sort things, make 3 piles
1 pile white
1 pile colored
1 pile work britches and rags.

To make starch, stir flour in cool water to smooth,
then thin down with boilin water.
Take white things, rub dirty spots on board, scrub hard,
and boil,
then rub colored. Don't boil just wrench and starch.
Take things out of kettle with broom stick handle,
then wrench, and starch.
Hang old rags on fence.
Spread tea towels on grass.
Pore wrench water in flower bed.
Scrub porch with hot soapy water.
Turn tubs upside down.

Go put on clean dress, smooth hair with hair combs.
Brew cup of tea,
sit and rock a spell and count your blessing.

Anonymous

# ~ 5 ~

▼

# ANNIE'S OFFER

The aroma of onions, from the simmering soup kettle setting on the backside of the wood stove, awakened a refreshed man. Jocko was hungrier than he realized. Smells from the dried ground sweet potatoes, boiling in the coffee pot, filled the cabin, and he smiled. During his time in the Union Army, sweet potato coffee had become a staple drink, and he recognized the sweet smell here in Annie's cabin. He felt better every time he woke up, and he knew he would be strong enough to leave very soon. He had to talk to Annie today.

Annie looked at Jocko as he slurped up the last of the soup with a chunk of her wheat bread. *When he starts getting restless, I'll know he'll be on his way.* She cleared the table; refilled their coffee cups and pushed the sugar bowl towards him. He reached in and took a couple of lumps only to put them into his shirt pocket.

"These are for Charlie," he said, when he saw Annie's quizzical look. "We talked about my staying on here for a while, and I still think it is a fine idea. How about you?"

Annie looked about the small cabin that held one double bed, one rocking chair, one kitchen table, several wooden chairs, a cook stove, a wood heating stove, and a pantry attached off the kitchen. Could they live together in this small space?

She held up her right hand in the stop position. She was afraid to speak for fear her voice would betray her true feelings. She wanted Jocko to stay around. She liked the company, and the feeling she was needed. She loved hearing him praise her, appreciate her. She also knew when he left part of her would go with him. A bond had grown over the past several weeks, and she was going to miss the companionship. Jocko noted a pensive look cross over Annie's face.

"I have a plan, Annie. Now hear me out." He took a sip of the hot coffee. "You make the best coffee I've ever tasted, and the way I see it, I owe you a great debt. You saved my life." He paused and looked at Annie, who was staring straight into his eyes. "I would like to work for you for a while and pay off my medical bill. If you would give me room and board, we can strike up a good deal for the both of us."

"Okay. What's your plan?"

- - - - - - -

"Annie, I'm going to be leaving here in the morning." Jocko looked out the window at the old tree stump that served as a bench.

"I'll make arrangements for another fellow to take over my job as camp meat supplier, just as soon as I get back to my place up near Stump Town." Jocko drummed his fingers on the kitchen tabletop.

"I'll leave here early in the morning, get to Philipsburg by late evening, and pack up a few things to bring back with me." As an afterthought, he said, "Why don't you make me up a list of supplies, and I'll bring them back with me? Maybe I could take the wagon and team, and leave Charlie here for you?"

"So you think I can read and write do you?" Annie laughed at her remark, and then wished she hadn't called attention to the difference in their backgrounds and race.

"In case you are wonderin', I was a slave on one of the largest plantations in the South, and my mother was an inside maid and cook. She made sure I learned how to clean, and dust, and polish the silver before I was three years old. My mistress and the mastah insisted that their domestic help know how to read and write. Not the same for the fieldslaves, though."

Annie stood up and went to a cupboard cabinet where she took out a small tablet and a pencil. She returned to the table and demonstrated her writing abilities by spelling out her name. AGNES MORGAN in block letters. "My mastah named me 'Agnes', but my mama, she called her baby girl 'Annie.'"

"I'm impressed. Did you learn your doctoring skills as a child, too, then?

"Laws, yes. Early on I showed an interest in herbs and plants, and what they could do for our bodies. It jess come to me. By my teen years, the mastah's overseer would send for me whenever a field hand was hurt, or if a baby was bein' born out in the hovels they had to call home." She frowned. "I saw more than I ever care to remember out in those huts."

Jocko brought the conversation back to his leaving. He would return within the next week, and plan to stay until the jobs Annie assigned for him were done. Then, he and Annie could ride into Philipsburg with her vegetables and foodstuffs that she wanted to sell at Shodair's Green Grocery.

Annie started writing down her needed staples now that there was to be a man to feed. She wrote a long list, including: *flour, cubed sugar, soda, canned tomatoes, coffee, tea,* and *matches.*

Usually, Annie made the trip to town later in the fall, but with Jocko's offer to bring back the supplies, she would stay on the homestead and work.

Annie happily robbed her cookie jar to give the money to Jocko to pay for the supplies. She put the coins into a leather drawstring pouch. This money she collected from the fishermen, who gratefully paid her with a fifty-cent piece for cooking their fish after a day on the Rock Creek. Many camped out in the meadow, pitched a canvas tent, hobbled their horse, and enjoyed Annie's home-cooked meals, also included in that price.

The afternoon passed swiftly, all thought of a nap forgotten. She and Jocko went outside to check over the wagon. He would take it to haul back some of his personal belongings that he didn't want to leave at his cabin. Both were happy with the decision that Jocko would return to help with the necessary repairs.

Another chore, where Annie could use a farm hand, was when she ordered a pig to slaughter from the neighboring pig farm. That was on her list of chores for fall. She used everything but the oink from that pig. Hams she wrapped in a gauze cloth, and hung them from hooks in the ceiling of the root cellar. Slabs of bacon shared in that same space. Annie smoked her meats. *I could keep that man here until the end of the year*, thought Annie, and she smiled.

# Elk Stew

Cut up a chunk of Elk meat into bite sized pieces.
Flour the pieces of meat.
Drop them into a pan full of bacon grease
and brown all sides.

Put a lid on the pan and let the meat cook.
Pour some water or beef broth (if you have any) in the pan.

Add some pealed potato chunks, onion halves, carrots,
Squash, and turnips, any root vegetables you might have.

Toss in a pinch of salt and some pepper.
Drop in some Thyme or Bay leaves for flavor.

Let it simmer in lots of liquid until everything is tender.
If you have some wine, put in a cup full near the end.

Eat hot.

# ~ 6 ~

▼

# JOSEPH LEAVES

It was still dark when Jocko and Annie hitched up Bess and Bob to the old hay wagon. It would be a long, slow ride to Philipsburg. They had decided it best for Jocko to take the wagon to bring back his things from his shack. He would load the wagon with Annie's supplies; find some rough sawed lumber, nails and chicken wire.

Annie stood by the open gate. Bingo ran back and forth between the two of them, and finally settled in beside Jocko's leg. Jocko reached down and scratched the dog's head and chin.

"You take care of Annie and the place, now, Bingo. I'll bring you a couple of deer bones in a few days."

He climbed into the wagon, gave a "giddy-yap" and a slap to the horses hindquarters. The animals moved toward the open gate.

"Whoa! There, fellas." He tipped his hat to Annie. "I'll be back within the next week, Annie. I have to take care of some left over business of mine, but that'll be no problem." He patted his vest pocket. "The list and your money are safe in here."

Jocko heard Charlie whinnying in the corral and he winced at the sound.

"He thinks I'm abandoning him, Annie. I guess you will have to talk to him some more after I leave." He picked up the reins, released the brake handle and demonstrating his driving skills, drove the team through the gate.

"Bye, Annie. See you in a few days."

As the team lumbered on down the dirt road, Jocko felt like singing at the top of his voice, announcing to the whole countryside that he was happy. His backside, after lying around for a week, was already feeling a bit sore from sitting on the wagon seat. He had his trusty rifle alongside him, and he found himself looking for wild game to shoot for the mining camp cooks.

Annie had watched him drive away with her wagon and horses.

"Well, let's hope he is the honorable man I believe him to be, and I will see Bess and Bob again soon." She turned back into her yard. "Come on Bingo, we need to get some work done, but first I need another cup of coffee."

Annie was happy, too. She felt comfortable with the arrangement. She knew Jocko was a godsend, even for all the trouble he'd caused her.

As the man returned to health, he had proved his mettle by helping with easy chores… like bringing in the wood to replenish her wood box by the stove. He gathered eggs after releasing the chickens. The animals responded to his settling in, feeding the horses and cows that Annie had in her field.

Even her old dairy cow, Bossie, (and her calf) which kept her supplied with fresh milk, tolerated Jocko's milking style.

Annie had a routine that worked well. Jocko did not mess with trying to re-arrange that schedule. She liked that. It was important that she kept control of this boss-employee arrangement.

As busy as Annie kept herself, the days seemed to drag. A week had passed. *Maybe I got took? Naw. Quit thinkin' this way. He'll be back any day now. He jess ran into somethin' to take care of, that's all. Anyways, his horse is still in my corral, so that 'mounts to somethin' right there. He wouldn't leave Charlie behind.* Back and forth went this conversation with herself, and each evening she'd feel let down once again.

In his absence, she had set up a cot, and made a nice space for Jocko to sleep in the barn. She'd cleaned out the best and tightest corner, so he would not be affected by the wind. She reasoned that, he being a meat hunter, he was used to sleeping on the ground for most of the year round. Yes, this cot would suit him fine.

However, Annie continued to fuss. She found a couple of old orange crates and made a nightstand for Jocko. She cleaned and filled an old kerosene lantern, and set out some matches. She stopped finally, and took the time to take a look at what she had created for a room for Jocko. *This will do really nice. He'll be comfortable here. He can hang his hat on those hooks on the wall, and store his gear up off the dirt floor. Anything he wants to do, to make this his own place, he can. He'll probably bring a pile of hides to keep them safe 'til fall sales.*

"I'm goin' fishin', Bingo. You want to come with me?" Annie always went fishing when her frustrations mounted like they were now. "Some fresh trout for dinner is the answer to my ills today."

It dawned on her that she'd been talking a lot to Bingo these past days and was glad for his company.

"Charlie needs a good walk, too. He's gettin' lazy standin' around, doin' nothun' but eatin', and rollin' in clover, but that can jess wait another day. What you say, Bingo? The river's callin' me."

Walking Bridge - Rock Creek

## ~ 7 ~

▼

# JOCKO RETURNS

Annie heard every sound in the meadows. The birds singing early in the evenings always gave her great joy. Tonight the air was filled with the electricity of impending storms, and the singing she usually listened to at this time of the evening had stopped. She looked out the window of her small cabin, not seeing anything out of the ordinary. But, it did feel to her that the wind had picked up.

*A storm must be brewin'. I best go get the chickens gathered and the cows into the barn. Charlie is prancin' around, too. Best go check on the critters.*

Then she heard the jangle of the horses' harness.

"Bingo! It's Bess and Ben. Jocko! He's back. Oh! Laws! He's back." Annie ran to the gate and swung it wide. She and Bingo danced in joy as the team lumbered on through.

"Hey! Annie! I'm finally back, and bringing gifts."

Jocko called out, as he set the brake on the wagon wheels, and jumped to the ground. He gave Annie a big hug and swung her around. Then realizing he was being too familiar with his employer, he abruptly dropped her back to the grass.

"I've come loaded with supplies and everything on your list, including a few surprises you might not want to know about." He laughed when he saw the familiar stance…hands on her hips, feet apart. He playfully pulled off Annie's head wrap and tossed it into the air.

"Let's get the horses unhitched and fed. They are a great team, by the way, Annie. We've gotten to know each other very well this past week." He retrieved Annie's head cover, but not before teasing her a bit with it, handing it to her, then snatching it back.

Annie couldn't stop grinning. She was happy to help Jocko put the animals to pasture. Charlie nickered and pranced on his hooves waiting for Jocko to come over and talk to him, too.

The wind had begun to send a good message that the storm was coming right down the canyon and would hit the homestead within the hour.

"It's goin' to rain, Jocko. Let's get back into the cabin. You've got everything covered with canvas tarps and tied down with good ropes. It'll be okay while we wait out the storm."

"Let's take in the flour and sugar and salt, Annie. We don't want that to get wet." Jocko lifted back the tarp far enough to reach in and remove the sacks of staples. He handed them down to Annie, who made several trips to the kitchen. After returning and securing the tarp again, they ran for the cabin. Inside, the warmth and security it provided, left the storm to work its' way through the homestead.

"It's good to see you back, Jocko. I about gave up on you a couple of days ago, but decided to hang on for Charlie's sake."

Annie put water in the coffee pot, and gave the stew she had bubbling in the big pot a stir.

"Aaahhh, Annie. I smelled that stew a mile down the road. I'd crawl on my knees for a bowl full of your stew. Even the horses picked up their pace when they recognized the home place." Jocko stretched his body, and walked over to the window to gaze at the storm.

"Here it comes. It's raining so hard it looks like a pond already out there in the yard."

Annie poured him a cup of coffee and one for herself. Then she sat at the kitchen table.

"Come, tell me all about your trip. Were you able to find a meat hunter for the camp cooks at the mines?"

Jocko sipped the coffee, and then grinned at Annie.

"You know? I think everything is going so smoothly, that this is where I am supposed to be. Too bad I had to almost die to find it out, huh?"

"That's not funny. Did you tell your friends you have a new name, Jocko?" Annie waited for him to continue and when he didn't, she prodded him.

"Was the mill full of rough sawn wood for the coop? How about the mercantile store? Jocko, tell me."

"I will…if you quit talking for a minute, so's I can get a word in edgewise."

Annie jumped up and went to the kitchen counter. She cut some freshly baked bread, took down bowls from the shelf and filled them with the steaming stew. She carried it all to the table, slamming the bowls hard, and again sat down.

"Eat."

"Now…Annie."

Jocko ate.

"I'm sorry, Annie. It's just good to be here again, and this is the best meal I've had since I left here ten days ago."

"Apology accepted. Now...*talk* to me." Annie sat back into her straight-back chair. "I've not seen another soul or heard another voice since you left. Company is always a real surprise back here in this part of the Hog Back, and you have important things to tell me."

Jocko started by telling her of the wild game he spotted on the road to Philipsburg, and of the wild goats grazing high on the side of the mountain basking in the sunshine. He told her how well the team performed for him, and how the plans took shape once he got back to his own cabin.

"Signs of an early fall are everywhere, Annie. The trees are turning, and it is getting darker earlier, have you noticed?" Jocko took their bowls to the counter but he kept his knife. He wanted one more slice of that delicious bread, and he intended to slather it with butter.

"Jam's in the cupboard iffen you be needin' somethin' sweet."

And the storm rolled through, leaving in its wake downed grasses in the meadow. The birds once again sang their nocturnal songs.

"We best be unloading the supplies before it gets dark on us."

Jocko untied the ropes, they both pulled back the wet tarp, letting it drop off the end of the wagon, where they shook it. They put it over the fence, leaving it there until the next day when it would be thoroughly dried.

"Laws. What is all this stuff?"

"I told you I brought surprises." Jocko lifted off a large square metal box. "This is a perfect fish smoker. We can preserve lots of fish in here."

He handed her the things from her list and she made periodical runs into the cabin. Things of his ownership he unloaded and took into the barn.

"I see you made me up my own space in the barn. Thanks. That will suit me just fine." He walked to the hay meadow and found Charlie waiting for him. He carried a saddle blanket over to the horse.

"Charlie. Hello again, old boy. I told you I'd be back for you. You're all wet. Let me get you dry." He took his time working with the horse, talking to him, rubbing his huge body with the blanket. "Come morning, I'll give you a good brushing, and we'll go for a ride. I need a trip into the mountains and so do you." He slapped his horse on the rump, and Charlie sidestepped away, but not until he had reached into Jocko's vest pocket for the expected sugar lump.

Annie lit the lantern in the barn for Jocko.

"Yell iffen you need anythin', Jocko. I'm bushed and still have some inside chores to do. So, it's goodnight to you." She started to walk away, but turned back. "I'm so happy to see you again. and I'll be ready to start work after breakfast."

"Goodnight, Annie. There's more to tell you, but it can keep until the morn." Jocko walked into the barn, hung up his hat and gun holster, rested his rifle near the bed head and blew out the lantern. Lying there in total darkness, smelling the clean scents that always come in the meadow after a rain, he sighed. "I'm a very lucky man, I am."

# ~ 8 ~

▼

# WITH THE DAWN

Annie was dressed and had breakfast cooking way before the crowing of the rooster. *I wish I'd made arrangements for this first mornin'. I'll give him five more minutes and then I am bangin' a pan out in the yard.*

Jocko was also up and dressed, waiting for some kind of a sign he should go into the cabin. *It's really early yet. Guess I better wait out here until I see her moving about in the yard.*

He saw Annie fanning the screen door. *Well, there is my sign. Here I go as a hired hand. Room and board will be more than enough for what I owe Annie.*

"Morning."

Jocko let the screen door slam behind him. He stood on one foot, then the other, until he finally sat down at the kitchen table. In his hand he had a stack of mail for Annie. "I stopped at the post office for my mail, and asked for yours. They gave it to me."

"Mornin'."

Annie had a stack of hotcakes, fried eggs and bacon already on the table, and she poured coffee for both of them. She was surprised, and pleased that he had thought of her mail. She'd read it later.

"I'm excited about getting started. I know it isn't even daylight out, but there is a lot of preparation we have to do first, like clear out the spot where we plan to build the chicken coop."

"Well, Annie, first off I am taking Charlie for a ride. He has been lazy long enough and we both need a trip into the mountains. Sorry, but you will have to start without me for a couple of hours." Jocko downed more of the hotcakes before he stood up.

"I'll be back by mid-morning."

He walked out the door to the corral where Charlie stood, waiting for the promised ride into the mountains. Jocko needed the time to think over all the events that had occurred while in the Philipsburg area. He had worked fast to make arrangements with the camp cooks for their meat supply, and he had loaded the wagon with supplies from the mercantile store, the lumberyard, and his cabin. He needed a time out.

*Annie is going to be a slave driver.*

Jocko chuckled over his choice of words…Annie a slave driver.

*She needs help, that's for sure. I wonder how long she has lived out here, and how she got into these mountains in the first place.*

Jocko tightened the cinch on the saddle and gave Charlie a hard nudge with his knee. "Let's get this saddle on tight before I step into the stirrup and wind upside down underneath your swollen belly."

Charlie lifted one hind leg and struck out at Jocko as he tightened down the cinch strap.

"Okay, buddy, let's go." Bingo had been watching this whole ritual. He let out a quick bark as if asking to go along.

"You better stay here with Annie, Bingo. We'll think to ask her next time I take off, but not today." The dog slithered down on his haunches and obeyed, staying behind as man and horse splashed through the creek not too far from where Bingo had found Jocko.

Bingo stayed until he no longer heard the sounds from the leather saddle, and the horse's hooves hitting the gravel bar, located on the far side of the bank.

Sunrise on the homestead rose fast and warm. It pleased Annie that the garden had been watered thoroughly by the heavy rain the night before. She went back into the kitchen, found her chicken coop plan that she had drawn out many months before. *Today's the day things start to get done around here,* she thought.

By the time Jocko returned and put Charlie out to pasture, Annie had decided the exact spot for the chicken coop. They could get in two solid hours of work before stopping for a late lunch. Annie scanned the Montana blue sky, and was pleased that the storm clouds had all cleared off during the early morning. Working together, they could have the coop roughed in, and the chickens roosting in safety before nightfall.

Jocko dug a trench outlining the size of the structure. Annie wanted the edge of the chicken wire buried into the ground.

"Why do you want to bury the wire and run it up the sides of the building, Annie?"

"It's the only way I know of to keep foxes and skunks and weasels outside the fence, away from the chickens and eggs," she replied. "Critters can chew wood, and dig holes, but not if wire stops them."

Jocko pounded corner stakes where Annie directed, and they began hauling supplies to the site. Poles, for framing the door and supporting the corners, and twelve-inch-wide by eight-foot-long boards, passed quickly from the barn to the building site. Annie carried handsaws, nails, and rolls of chicken wire, hinges, and other tools.

By noon, Annie called a halt and went inside to make a lunch for them. She had sliced beef, layered between two thick slices of sour dough bread, iced tea, and hard boiled eggs ready when Jocko came in. His hands were washed, but sweat stains showed on his shirt.

"Annie, you're a hard-working woman. You amaze me at how you worked right along with me." He took a bite of a boiled egg. "Then you come inside and fix us a feast." He smiled at her as he took a drink of the sweet tea.

Annie cocked her head sideways. "I'm so happy to be workin' today, I'll keep side-by-side all day and, even if I'm achin', you'll never know it." She had pulled her skirt between her legs and pinned the cloth at her waist, using an oversized safety pin, the kind the Chinese laundrymen used on their cloth laundry bags. She wished she had a pair of men's pants to wear when working this hard, as it would give her the freedom she needed to move more easily.

Jocko laughed at her hastily made trousers. "Next time you go shopping, you better find some trousers, my girl."

Annie was surprised by what Jocko had called her. She jumped up from the chair. "Time's a wastin'." She grabbed her straw hat off the hook before she slammed the kitchen screen door behind her.

"Come away from the porch, Annie. The chicken coop isn't going anywhere. The chickens are wanting to settle down and go to sleep."

Jocko stretched. "I'm heading for the barn myself, and I'll make sure the horses have fresh water." He moved next to Annie.

"We made great progress and quick work of that chicken coop, didn't we? Tomorrow I'll hammer some nesting boxes together from the left over boards and you will have happy chickens. The roof will not take much more work. We need to do some trimming around the edges is all."

"Thank you Jocko. I'm goin' to turn in now, too. Tomorrow is another day, and we need sleep." She smiled, and gave him a little wave as he walked off the porch, and across the way to the barn.

"Goodnight."

"G'night. See you in the mornin'."

Jocko was so sore and tired. He pulled off his boots, but didn't light the lantern. He flopped on the top of the cot and was immediately asleep.

# ~ 9 ~

▼

# THE NEW CONTRACT

The days started before dawn and ended after darkness fell. A workable routine developed between the two as they toiled silently, keeping their focus on whatever the project at hand.

Jocko had been fixing fence by the river all morning. The sun beat down on his back as he dug postholes. The work was tough. Even the deer passing through the meadow went unnoticed by Jocko.

Whew! *I haven't worked this hard in a long time. I miss my mountains and hunting game.* Lost in his thoughts, he was surprised to hear a voice coming from behind him.

"Well, will you jess look at that? You have one more post to go, and we'll be stringin' the wire." Annie made a detour away from Jocko, and headed for the barn. She put on her canvas gloves and grabbed a roll of barbed wire that she had been storing for a couple of years.

"I'll bring the gate down too," she yelled back at Jocko. "We can get this here wire stretched out yet today, maybe even get one strand on."

Annie stood tall in the sunshine. Jocko kept digging the posthole.

"Bring me some water, will you please, Annie? This is tough going down here in this river soil. I hope the other side by the house and road isn't this hard to dig." He kept on working while Annie filled a tin cup that she kept on a nail by the well pump handle. She carried it to Jocko.

"Thanks Annie. Aaahhha. That tasted mighty good." Jocko wiped his brow with the back of his sleeve. "I could use another cup, if you would bring it, please?"

- - - - - - -

That evening Annie and Jocko sat comfortably on the porch, bone tired, but content with the amount of work they had completed in the last seven days. The sun had not set yet. The birds were flying hither and yon, putting on a wonderful aerial show. Bingo was sleeping at the end of the porch. Neither had anything to discuss. Finally, Jocko broke the silence.

"Annie, we have really made some great changes, haven't we? Look over yonder at how clean the area is where a dumping ground used to be. Just look at that fence, nice and taut. Why you could play a violin bow acrost those wires and make music."

He laughed as Annie had jumped up, pretending to play a violin on her left shoulder. Wanting to join in on the celebration, Bingo barked and danced around on his hind legs. He bumped into Jocko, and then Annie, until she grabbed him by the collar to calm him down.

Then Jocko turned serious. "You see that old sawmill over there near those trees? Why I've been checking it out, and with a bit of oil on the parts, I think I can get that up and running. We could cut trees off your hillside, bring them down here, rough cut them, and make you a much better barn, twice the size, fix the roof on the house, and…"

Annie interrupted him with dreams of her own. "How about draggin' up river rock and buildin' us a fireplace? We could build another room, too."

They both stopped talking and stared at each other.

"Jocko, would you want to stay on the rest of this fall? I can surely use your help, and we get along real well."

"I thought you'd never ask." Jocko had been pondering over this very plan but didn't want to seem like a moocher to Annie.

"I'll stay and help you harvest the garden, and we can take the wagon load to Philipsburg. There is still one more cutting in the hay field that you are going to need for feed, come winter." There was enough work for two men.

Annie stood up, walked over to Jocko and shook his hand. "It's settled. I am happy with our new arrangement. Sure hope you keep likin' my cookin' cause that's all I can offer you for all your hard work."

Jocko, happy with the way the conversation had gone, favorably towards him and his future, said, "Annie, the river's calling. Let's go catch us some fish for supper."

He reached out his hand and took hers, and together they walked off the porch. Annie kept her pole and creel leaning against the porch most all summer, and whenever stresses, or some free time showed up, she was off fishing.

"We can catch a mess of fish for our late supper, sure thing."

Since Jocko lost his fishing pole, when he fell into Rock Creek, he had purchased himself a fine rod and reel in Philipsburg at Winestein's Mercantile, on his trip after being so ill with the typhoid fever.

Fishing and hunting for a living had served him well. He preferred being out of doors. Catching fish had always come easy for him, even as a youngster on the family farm in New Jersey.

*Some day I'll have to tell Annie my life story, maybe this winter, iffen she keeps me around that long.*

Bingo kept right at their side. It was a grand way to end their very busy workweek.

▼

# MARRIAGE PROPOSAL

Joseph and Annie continued the rest of that late summer to work in harmony. Neither was willing to admit to the feelings building for each other. He slept in the barn, and kept good counsel. She cooked the meals and kept his clothes clean. But they were sharing more than these basic needs. They were living a life and building a future in the never-ending work that needed to be done on the homestead.

The nights had become chillier, and the morning grass held the dew longer. Annie decided on September 7th as the day they would take the loaded wagon to Philipsburg to market her garden produce. She packed hand knit sweaters, scarves, hats and mittens for sale, as well as rag rugs.

"Jocko, iffen you'd pack all the squash, cabbage, and onions that are stored in the root cellar, we'd have a head start on the loadin'," announced Annie. "I think we'll dig up the potatoes today, and get them dried off before we sack them up in the flour sacks you'll find in the old section of the barn.

"Oh! There's an old piece of chicken wire in there, too, for us to lay the potatoes on so's they can dry off proper." She thought a moment. "We'll dig the carrots and clean off some of the dirt and put them on the wire, too."

"Will get to it, Annie. But first, I've got a question for you."

Jocko knelt down on one knee on the plank floor. "Annie, will you marry me? Its getting colder nights now, and freezing rain is going to start in another week. I want to move into the cabin with you." Jocko put on a hangdog expression, and Annie laughed right out loud.

"Why, you old fool. No. I won't marry you, and you know why. You're white and I'm colored. Haven't you noticed that in all these weeks you been out here stuck with me?" Annie walked over and gave him a playful smack on the side of his head. Then she held out her hand to him and he stood up.

"You built that extra room on to the house for yourself, didn't you?"

She watched Jocko's head bob up and down.

"Well, then, I'd say you better move your stuff into it." Annie dropped her head and stared at her shoes.

Jocko walked the few steps between them, and took Annie into his arms. She did not resist, but nestled into his embrace and rested herself against his muscled chest, enjoying the feeling of his strong arms encircling her lean frame.

"Annie, sometimes man's laws are really stupid. I do care for you deeply, and I've been meaning to ask you for a while now…about my staying on here through the winter…and always." He sighed as he continued to hold her close.

"We make a good team, you and I. Old gal, I feel real happy inside. What you say we marry each other right here in the cabin?"

Surprised, Annie looked up into his eyes.

"I want you to stay, Jocko. The best thing I've done in a long, long time was to fish you out of that there river. Let's wait until we get back from Philipsburg for any kind of a ceremony, okay?" Annie moved away from the comfort of Jocko's arms.

"Let's go dig potatoes."

Annie started for the door.

"By the way, Jocko, that was the nicest proposal a gal like me ever got." With that she was back to her usual self, headed for the garden where the tools were all lined up, hanging on a board in the newly built shed.

Annie smiled and sang all morning long. She had an idea to present to Jocko later that evening.

- - - - - - -

"Don't you ever get tired of eatin' my stews?"

"Naw! You are working too hard to be concerned with cooking other meals. We get good, healthy food right from this here land; fish from that river flowing right by your front door, and meat from the deer that wander through. Annie, we have it all right here on the homestead."

"That brings me to what I want to talk to you about, and I want to bring it up now. Jocko, if you want to stay, you are welcome to all I have, includin' my bed. And you know I am happy with all the work you have done on the place. It looks like a proper farm from the road, with all the fences up tight. The icehouse is all sealed real good, and the squirrels won't be gettin' into this house come winter. Look at the sheds we have and the new outhouse. Even the wagon has its' own space." She laughed and Jocko sat, waiting for her to finish speaking.

"Here's what I want to do. When we go to Philipsburg in a couple of days, I want to visit Judge Durfee, and draw up new papers on this homestead. I want to include your name right along with mine and call this the Morgan-Case Homestead. That way, if somethin' should happen to me, you would have the place for your own. Laws! Look at all the work you have done out here."

Joseph was shocked and he didn't know what to say. He never expected this generous offer to come his way.

"Annie. I….I am speechless. I…I don't know what to say. It is such a generous offer on your part. You know why I stayed on here. I owe you, not you owe me."

"Well, yes, in the beginnin'. But we've moved way on past that time. Iffen you want to stay with me, I want you to be a partner on the land. You know about the trees on the hillside, where the boundary markers are, and you deserve a home right along with me." She reached over and took Jocko's hand, covering his rough, calloused fingers with her equally rough and calloused hands.

"We make a good team, Jocko. Even though I can't marry you by the laws of Montana Territory, I can and will marry you in my heart. Let's call that good enough and do a 'strike-a-deal' handshake on it."

Jocko moved his belongings into the cabin that night. Annie poured glasses of homemade grape wine, and she and Jocko celebrated each other.

## ~ 11 ~

▼

# TRANSPORTING EGGS

"What's all that bangin' goin' on in the barn?" asked Annie when Jocko came in for a break.

"Banging? I don't hear anything." Jocko smiled as he swung himself into the wooden kitchen chair. "I came in 'cause I smelled cookies. Sure enough, I was right. Uumm… good ones, too." Jocko bit into an oatmeal raisin cookie, still warm from the oven and arranged in a nice row on the plate. Annie poured him a cup of his favorite coffee and sat down next to Jocko.

"We need to figure out how we's goin' to fit everythin' into the wagon for the trip to Philipsburg in a couple of days, you know?"

"Don't fret so, Annie. It'll all go just fine. Wait and see."

With that Jocko reached for his cap, gave her a pat on her shoulder and returned to the privacy of the barn.

Once again Annie heard banging. *What's he up to? When he shuts the door, I know that means I am to stay out. So, stay out I will. At least I know he is busy doin' somethin'.*

Jocko worried about transporting the fragile eggs. When coming out West back in the 1870s, Jocko had been amazed at a prairie schooner one of his army buddies had purchased for the journey with his family to the Dakota Territories. A special swing hung from the cross rafters that supported the canvas cover. In this swing were all the fragile items his wife wanted with her.

Everything she held dear, figurines, dolls and violins, she would not leave behind. Wrapping them in pillows and blankets was the way most travelers packed, but it was not usually successful. Even spring wagons were hard to ride in, and fragile items cracked. Many tears were shed over the loss of a beloved doll.

Jocko was making Annie an egg crate swing holder that would be the best way to get her eggs to town. Every cracked egg was a wasted egg, and Jocko knew how important it was for Annie to get every penny she could. She candled every egg when preparing them for storage. She had them upright in crates, but that would not assure her that the eggs wouldn't break over the twenty-five miles of rough road to town. Past trips had, indeed, cost her many eggs.

The banging sounds could not be helped and, at this point, he really didn't care if Annie came in and saw what he was doing. He knew it was a good idea that would work well. He had gathered short pieces of leftover poles from the lumber pile. The first thing he did was take a hatchet and notch the ends of the poles part ways, so that when he nailed them together, he had a strange looking arc, or a rib, three inches wide and eight feet long, resembling a rainbow. This rib he double-nailed to the inside of the wagon box to form the arc that would support the tarp that he intended to put over the top of the load.

To the middle of this arc, he had wrapped two strands of rope, about a foot apart, from each other on the rib. He pushed the now four strands of rope through a board that he had carved out holes. Next, he knotted the rope ends on the bottom of the boards.

*Well, would you look at that? This here is some egg crate holder. It's time to show Annie.*

Jocko shouted back towards the cabin.

"Annie, come out here will you? I've got a surprise for you."

Annie hurried outside and into the barn. She was curious as to what he had been up to all morning, and now she'd finally find out.

"What's that?" Annie stood stock still with her hands on her hips.

She stared at the contraption, not having a clue as to what Jocko had been wasting his time on building.

"Here. Hold this end, will you?" He fussed with the swing ropes. "Hand up something I can set in the basket, and we'll test out my job."

Annie looked about the barn and found an empty crate. She handed it to Jocko who put it into the rope swing. He then gave the ropes a push, and together they watched the swing in the back end of the wagon.

"Annie, this here is your egg holder. Yes, Ma'am. We'll set your box of eggs right in this here swing, and you won't have a broken egg this trip. No siree." Jocko was so proud of himself that Annie had to laugh.

"You old fool, I think you have somethin' here. We'll test it. You can put your hides on the wagon bed and then hang this egg swing over them near the tail gate." She frowned. "Are you sure the arc can take the weight of all them eggs?"

The last thing Annie needed was broken eggs all over the other vegetables and goods they would have crammed into every inch of space.

"I'm thinking of making two ribs, Annie. If I had metal it would be secure for sure, but two wooden arcs will be strong enough." Jocko jumped down out of the wagon box and gave Annie a big hug. "No harm in giving it a try, anyways."

▼

# Preparation

"Hey! Wait for me to help you." Jocko watched Annie take another load of stuff to the side of the wagon, parked the night before by the cabin door. He pulled on his boots, and didn't stop for a jacket. He helped Annie inside the wagon as he handed her another sack of potatoes. She stacked the burlap sack into a small space, not wasting an inch of the wagon-floor bed.

"Brrr. It's cold this morning. Good thing we plan to leave today after breakfast." He looked to the clouds hanging low. "Last thing we want is to get caught in a snowstorm this early in the season."

Departure date of September 7th came upon them faster then expected. Up before dawn, Annie had been loading the wagon alone. Since Jocko would be driving the team, she left him to sleep until he woke up.

The wagon was nearly full. Crated eggs waited to be loaded, along with the jugs of sour cream, home churned butter, and freshly killed chickens. This was the end result of their hard work. Whatever money Annie made on this trip to town, it would be all she'd have to show for the untold hours of labor.

Storing enough food for her…and now Jocko…was a challenge for Annie, but she figured this winter would work out fine for them both. She always managed to come through the cold months with a bit of excess in the root cellar. She had her root vegetables, her herbs, and her canned goods, all lined up looking like a beautiful rainbow of colors. The excess from her huge over-an-acre-sized garden was what she was able to take to town every fall.

This year was a cinch with Jocko's help with the weeding, canning and storing of things properly. A row of smoked hams and bacon, hanging from the rafters of the root cellar, was a welcome and comforting sight.

Jocko went to the old barn and carried back his stored hides and loaded them onto the tail end of the wagon. "Let's eat. I need coffee."

But, before he entered the cabin, he walked to the meadow and called over the horses, while shaking a pail of oats. He gave them fresh water from the well, and patted them on their massive necks.

"Charlie, you better get in on this too. You are going to be left alone with Bossie and her calf for a couple of days, but we'll be back." He worried about the cow not being milked, but she would keep the calf happy, and it couldn't be helped. They would not be gone any longer than necessary.

He looked over at Bossie contentedly chewing her cud, while her calf stood off by herself on the other side of the field. Bossie, a very large Jersey cow, had deer-like round eyes, and sported the prettiest eyelashes on any cow Jocko had ever seen. She had a set of horns that gave her a "crown" look, and she could use those horns for defense should a coyote come around disturbing her or her calf.

Bossie gave more than enough milk every day for Annie's use. Annie let the milk sour on occasion and made cottage cheese. She'd put the curds into a cheesecloth bag and hang it up on a hook she had screwed in over the counter top. A huge bowl caught the drippings. When she had squeezed all the moisture out of the bag, she'd dump the curds into the emptied bowl. Next, she'd stir in sweet cream. Only then was it ready to eat, and Jocko enjoyed every bite of the handmade treat. The curd was a good seller at Shodair's Green Grocery, and Annie made sure she had plenty of it to sell.

Annie wasted nothing in her kitchen. Even the chickens benefited from the sour cream when occasionally she would dump some of it into a low trough for them to drink.

Bossie had such a high cream content that making butter was easy. Annie drank buttermilk on hot summer days. Jocko hand-churned the butter paddles around and around, waiting for his glass, too. Butter, wrapped in cheesecloth, was stacked in the icehouse where it could freeze in the winter and stay cool in the summer. Annie needed butter for all of her year-round baking. She did not use much lard, except from bacon grease she kept in a jar with a rubber stopper in the cupboard. Known throughout the county for her baked goods, Annie kept the fact that she always used fresh butter her very own secret from the ladies.

For a small homestead, this one proved more than self-sufficient. Even with Jocko added to the household, there was more than enough produce and other products to completely fill the wagon.

# ~ 13 ~

▼

# September 7

Jocko still had to load the food Annie had packed for the trip. There would be several rest stops along the way, coming and going. Annie sometimes slept under the wagon on past trips, but they would make it in one long day this time.

He'd like to take her to the Silver Lake Hotel and Restaurant in Philipsburg, but he knew two things would stop him. One, it was an expensive place to stay, and two, she was 'a colored,' and would not be allowed inside the doors. Instead, they would camp in his cabin near Stump Town. Annie had, on other occasions, camped out in the designated campground, across the street from the hotel.

They would keep the horses on tethers while attending to their business, since it cost $2.00 a day per horse to set them up in Hammond's Livery Stable. Bingo would be on a leash, not able to wander or get into a dogfight with a town dog.

They were going to take Bingo with them, because a mountain lion had left scat near the house, and the tracks

Jocko found were large. Bingo would be free lunch if Jocko weren't there to shoot the lion. The animal had been brazen enough to come near the cabin when they were home. It surely would attack the dog if he were left behind.

The few setting hens and the one rooster, left in the now secure coop, would do just fine until their return. Jocko saw to it that water filled several buckets, and he spread some chicken feed on the ground floor.

"You old biddies better be good, or Annie will have you in with the dumplings." They clucked softly at Jocko as if to say, "No, she won't. She likes our eggs too much."

"At last I smell bacon. My growling stomach is ready for whatever Annie has on my plate."

Jocko walked back towards the cabin a very contented man. He and Annie were compatible, had a good work relationship, and they were friends. They both were looking forward to this trip to Philipsburg, as long and hard, as it was to make the journey. Interestingly enough, they both had their own reasons for making the trip besides selling their wares.

Annie had a shopping list for yarns and material, and household items. She made most everything she needed, like soap. She added jar rings to her list.

Her other list, the one for Jocko to take to the hardware mercantile store, was growing longer daily: Matches, small hatchet, handsaw, punches, and a hand-drill joined the other items.

If she made enough money, she wanted to shop for a new pair of boots. *Well, at least new tie strings*, she thought. *I could get me a pair of trousers, maybe?*

She craved fresh fruit, thinking of oranges, plums and grapes. She planned to bring back crates full of grapes to make wine.

Her raspberry bushes and apple trees were harvested now, and proof of that was loaded in the wagon. She had spent several days filling jars with applesauce and sealing the lids. She left dried apple slices in the pantry, and she had solid apples set aside in the sand box that she kept in the root cellar. These apples she intended to use during the winter months in pies, especially at Christmas time.

Another craving for Annie was books. She loved to read out loud in the evenings when the snow fell outside the window, closing her in for months. While visiting with Judge Durfee, she'd ask to check out a few of his books from his private library. She had a stack of books to return to him. This ritual came about years ago when she worked for Judge Durfee and displayed her love for reading. Books to purchase were out of her grasp, and the Judge generously loaned her books, knowing she would be responsible to see they were returned to him.

Her list always grew long over the interim between trips to town. Annie wanted to visit with other women, and hoped to meet some of them in the grocery store or the mercantile store. She wanted some womanly gossip, too.

Annie was the only ethnic woman in town, so her "friends" were limited and rather standoffish until they got to know her. Even then, she was not invited to many private events in town. Annie, used to this treatment, paid little heed to it.

Jocko had his own list of supplies. His list noted items needed to keep the tools sharpened, and feed for the horses, chickens and the dairy cow. His personal wants were few, as he only on occasion smoked a pipe. His fondness for sweets would send him into the local candy store, where he would also purchase nuts. Later in the evening, he and Annie would stop in at a couple of pubs and have a pint or two of warm beer.

He, too, looked forward to this trip to town. He hoped to be able to find something special for Annie for a Christmas present. What that would be he wasn't sure, but he knew he'd know it when he saw it.

Jocko enjoyed visiting with his old friends, and he wanted to find out how the meat hunters were working out for the mine cooks. The mines continued to operate in the winter months. Jocko was pleased with the turn of events in his life. He had a warm and happy place to spend this winter.

He would take Annie to his cabin up near Stump Town, and make sure things were still secure. He left the door unlocked at all times, and he always left canned food on the counter, just in case somebody needed it as a refuge. Occasionally, the postman left a notice for mail on the table, but usually Jocko collected it himself at the post office when he was in town.

Jocko received a pension from the United States government for his time spent in the services of the Union Army during the Civil War. There were times when that check was what kept Joseph Case alive.

Jocko could not remember being called 'Joseph' after he came west. For some reason he was nicknamed "Fisher Jack by the railroad men" and it stuck. But, Annie had changed his name once again to "Jocko" and that would remain his nickname for the rest of his life.

When he had arrived back in town after being so ill, he mentioned that Annie Morgan had given him a name of "Jocko" as a joke. And he knew when he entered the Bucket of Blood Saloon in Philipsburg tomorrow, he'd hear his new name shouted out by the old cronies that lingered there nursing a mug of beer. *It will be great to share some stories again,* he thought.

- - - - - - -

"I'll have Bess and Ben hooked to the wagon by the time you tidy up the kitchen, Annie. Then you can grab your straw hat, and we'll be on our way. Oh, and if you'd bring our heavy outerwear, we are going to need them both directions, I'm thinking."

Annie smiled. She had several wool blankets, boots, wool socks, Jocko's rifle and sidearm, and other supplies laid out on the bed.

*Needin' a jacket. Laws! How did that man ever take care of himself before now? We be needin' beddin' and food for three days, jugs of water, and a lunch for today when we stop by Willow Creek to let the horses rest up a bit. He's goin' to think I'm movin' out of the cabin when he comes back in to help me load up all this stuff, but I ain't goin' without it.*

With everything finally packed, she slammed her cabin door. She, too, never locked the door. "For iffen someone needs to get inside, I don't want them breakin' the glass window. It's too precious to replace." She had told Jocko this story one night when they returned from fishing on the river and he had found the door unlocked.

Annie whistled to Bingo to jump onto the tailgate. She raised it up, latching it securely with an iron bar through the loops at both ends of the wagonbed sides. She walked over to the extra wide gate and swung it open.

"Gee up, and haw!" shouted Jocko as he released the wagon brake. This started the team to move. With a "Gee Up" and a pull on the right rein, he expertly drove the team through the sharp right turn onto the county lane. He waited for Annie to catch up.

"We're finally on our way to Philipsburg. We'll soon be eating ice cream from the Doe Brothers Ice Cream Parlor, and drinking beer at the saloon. Think we be needin' anythin' else?"

Jocko laughed as he clicked the team into moving on down the dirt road. He remembered then what he had forgotten he needed. A pillow to sit on, but he decided not to go back for it.

Annie reached under her wood seat.

"Surprise! Look what I have for us." She held up pillows and promptly plopped one beneath herself and handed one to Jocko who, without skipping a beat, stood up for the welcomed pillow.

"See Annie, that's why I love you. You just take such good care of me. You think of everything."

Dawn was breaking as they rode towards the streaked colors in the Montana blue sky. Deer, feeding in the early morning grasses, didn't even bother to run off into the trees, but gave a silent nod to the humans passing through.

"All's well with us," said Annie as she reached her arm over to link it with Jocko's, if only for a few minutes. Little did she know that Mouser, her barn cat that never came near the cabin, had jumped into the wagon during all the loading, and decided, as cats are prone to do, to ride along.

Mouser and Bingo tolerated each other's space. But, this long journey might be the undoing of that. Bingo would surely discover the cat, curled up asleep on top of the stack of blankets.

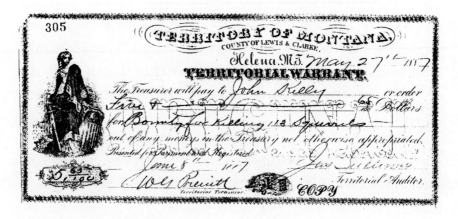

# ~ 14 ~

▼

# Day in Philipsburg

Jocko slept soundly in his cabin near Stump Town. Earlier, he had turned the team of horses into his small corral, making sure they were fed and watered, after pulling the wagon some twenty-five miles. It had been a long day, and sleep came easily. Even Bingo was curled up asleep at the side of the bed.

Annie had started a fire in the wood-burning cook stove as soon as they had arrived. She tossed together a hurried meal of cooked ham and the farl of bread she'd packed, knowing it would be needed for their dinner.

She had rummaged through Jocko's cupboard, and found some ground chicory nuts that would do for coffee. Jocko left behind staples just in case someone came by, needing food and a place to get in out of a storm. Many times Jocko had found a penciled note on his wood table, thanking him for dinner.

Annie sighed as she watched Jocko sleep. *How easily sleep comes to him. He must have a good heart, and a clear conscience to be able to drift off like that. How I wish my mind would shut off tonight, too.*

But, Annie had things to do before she could crawl under the wool blankets and close her eyes. She had to organize her lists for what she wanted to sell, and what she wanted to buy in the morning. Just the thought of being in Philipsburg where the stores full of merchandise, and pretty things to look at, was enough to keep any woman awake. She hoped she'd meet some of her women friends, and that there would be time for them to visit, and catch her up on the latest town gossip. Usually, several of the ladies would be shopping while she shopped.

A beautiful crisp-air fall morning, filled with the sound of birds singing woke up the couple.

"Jocko, we are wasting half the day. Get up...*Get up*! We have to go." Annie was pulling on her long dress, talking as she went about her morning toilet of washing her face in the cold water she had set out the night before in a pitcher and bowl set. The cold splash hit her face and opened her eyes wide.

"Hurry." Bingo was barking at the commotion, and Annie opened the door to let him out. Jocko, by now had pulled on his britches and socks, and he stuck his feet into his boots. He hopped on one foot while pulling on the other boot as he headed for the door. While he hitched up the team to the tarp-covered wagon, Annie made a quick breakfast of bread, fried eggs, bacon and coffee.

"Jocko, let's *go*. I can't wait another second."

"It's good to see you so excited, Annie. I hope you make good money today at the Shodair Green Grocery. I'll have you drop me off at Freyschlag, Huffman and Company store. I'll take my hides off the wagon, and you can then go on over to the grocery store. When you finish up you can come back and pick me up, along with the supplies I'll collect, if you leave me your list."

As Bob and Bess turned up the dirt road that led into the town, a golden glow from the now risen sun, spread before them. It cast a silhouetted black shadow of the horses as they made their way up the street. The storefront windows seemed to sparkle with an eerie light, as if Annie and Jocko were entering into a magic city. Annie clapped her hands in sheer delight. She could not hold back her excitement and joy at being in the nearest town to her Hog Back Mountain homestead. It had been at least nine months since she had been to town.

Even though they were early, many of the store front doors were blocked open with a big rock. Some of the store clerks waved to them when they heard the jangling wagon pass, then they returned to sweeping the dust from their wooden sidewalks. Annie waved and smiled back. She kept one hand in the thick fur around Bingo's neck, as she didn't want him to jump from the wagon.

Their first stop found the Freyschlag, Huffman and Company store open.

"I'll catch up with you later, Annie." Jocko unloaded the large pile of hides, and stacked them up by the huge double doors on the backside of the building. He smiled as Annie clicked the reins and drove off, never looking back. She had places to go and people to see.

Jocko had people to see and places to go on his own. He hoped to be able to do some shopping for Christmas presents, to find surprises for Annie.

"Well, first things first." Jocko walked into the cool, darkened interior of the building. "Hello. Anybody working today?"

"Jocko. So, you *are* still alive. Rumors are you were dead all these weeks. Where you been? Hunting game, were you?"

Jocko laughed as he stretched out his hand for a handshake from Huffman. The men said their 'good morning' greetings. Then they walked outside to bring in the stack of hides.

"I usually do buy your hides later in the year, Jocko. What's the occasion for selling now?" asked Huffman.

"I need some money, friend. I am hoping you might have some trade items in stock even though it is pretty early in the season." Jocko had started to spread out the hides, putting animals of like kind together in stacks. He had mostly beaver hides, since he had run a trap line on both the South Fork, and on Burr Creek. Both streams had beavers since their water pooled at the oxbows and didn't run as fast all year long like Rock Creek did. Jocko knew how to properly clean a hide, keeping the fur fresh looking and firm, just the way the traders liked to find them. Hides still sold well at the Pacific Hide and Fur Co. in Butte.

The traders sold to back east hide buyers, and the money doubled with each transaction. Jocko would be paid $3.00 per pound for his beaver pelts, Huffman would get $6.00 a pound, and the trader in the East would pay $12.00 a pound to the dealer from Pacific Hide and Fur. The demand for beaver hats for gentlemen was a fashion fad, selling daily in the haberdashery shops in New York City and Boston. The line of sale didn't stop there, however. Londoners and European gentlemen demanded beaver pelts for top hats as well.

Buffalo, elk, deer, moose, mountain lions, beaver, steer, as well as fox and minx, rounded the mound now checked and ledgered into Huffman's account book. The morning moved quickly as the two men dickered back and forth. Finally, a tally was reached that met both their expectations. Jocko, keeping his feelings close to the vest, hid his happiness at the total amount of money he had collected in cash and in trade.

What he would use his credit for filled his thoughts as he walked through the merchandise. He picked up tools, knowing he needed a drill. Off to the side, Jocko spotted a most wonderful machine. Something he had not seen for many years.

"Would you look at that? Isn't that a Singer sewing machine?" Jocko walked over to examine it more closely. He turned the right hand crank and the wheel easily whirled around.

"By golly! This is just what I want for my girl." He turned around to face the storeowner. "How much for the sewing machine? Does it come with all its parts ready to go?" He waited rather impatiently as Huffman fiddled with the tag.

"We just got this beauty in yesterday afternoon. You are the first one to see it unpacked and set up. Give it a try. The needle is in it and it stitches like a well-oiled machine." He smiled at Jocko. "What do you want with one of these anyway? You going to start making leather vests or something?"

Jocko gave him a sideways glance as he squatted on his heels in front of the machine. *What a wonderful surprise this would be for my girl. Now I am going to wheel and deal.*

"How much?"

"Well, now, don't you want to hear about all the features?

"No. How much?"

Again Huffman fiddled with the price tag. He knew Jocko was interested. He decided to get as much as he could for this new-fangled machine. "Why, Jocko, this here sewing machine is going to change women's lives all over the West." Huffman paused and looked at Jocko.

The frontier was developing with so many people pouring into the territories all over the West now that the Indian wars were coming to an end.

The capture of Sitting Bull and Cochise had opened the floodgates for the "Westward Ho!" movement. Wagon trains arrived almost daily into Helena and Butte. Virginia City boasted a population of over thirty-five thousand population, with mostly men working the mines.

Women also got caught up in the excitement of opening up the towns in the western territories. School teachers, store keepers, boarding house keepers, to name a few occupations for women, brought a better class of living to the towns, now springing up like mushrooms after a heavy rain.

The price tag on the sewing machine read $60.00. That included all of the necessities of needles, rulers, gauges, oil, a bobbin, instructions, a red case to keep all of the supplies safe and in one place, and the belts needed to attach the sewing head to the treadle operated by the sewer's right foot under the cabinet. Three small drawers were built in to the right side of the cabinet.

"If you just want the sewing machine head, I can let that go for about $40.00." Huffman paused. "You could make the cabinet if you bought the proper tools." He grinned. "Maybe this machine will take the mountain man out of the mountains and turn you into a cobbler or something."

Jocko did not hesitate. He knew this was the Christmas present for Annie.

"No. No. I want the whole outfit." Jocko put his arm around Huffman's shoulder. "Let's take a look in your ledger book, and see how I did with the hides." He knew he could make the trade, and have money left over to spend on the supplies he had on his list. They struck a deal favorable to each party.

"You robber," said Jocko jokingly. "I'll take it. Will you help me wrap it in a tarp? I don't want Annie to see it when she comes back to load up the supplies."

As an afterthought he said, "I want to keep this a secret from my girl, Huffman. This is going to be a Christmas present for Annie Morgan. I'm spending the winter out at her homestead, and, well, you might as well be the first to congratulate me. Annie and I, well, we are going to hitch up common law like, over at Judge Durfee's office later this afternoon." *Annie will be flabbergasted when she finds out about this.*

Huffman stared. "Why you old son-of-a-gun. Found you a place to get in out of the winter storms did you?" He slapped Fisher Jack on the back. "Annie is one fine woman. She sure did take good care of Judge Durfee's uncle out there in that cabin." He wrote something down on another page of the huge ledger that kept all of his accounts, sales and trades on a daily basis.

"I don't know if you are aware, but Annie worked here in town for the Judge in his office, and she also worked at his mansion, too. The Durfees think the world of her." He smiled up at Jocko. "She needs a helping hand, Fisher Jack, and you're just the man to be that extra pair of hands. I am happy for the two of you."

"By the way, I have a new name. Annie calls me Jocko and I like it." He looked at the storeowner. "From here on out, I'm answering to that."

Huffman walked over to a front counter and pulled out a tray of rings. "Seems to me you will be needing one of these." He held up a solid gold band.

"Just look at that. Yes. This is my lucky day. Add it to my bill. It looks large enough. You know Annie has worked hard, and she has large hands. I'll try it on me for size." Jocko slid the ring up to his second knuckle where it lodged. "Yep. This will just fit her fine."

The storeowner put the ring into a small black velvet box, snapped the hinge holding the top, and handed it to Jocko. Jocko slid the little box into his vest pocket and patted it.

"What a surprise this will be for my girl."

The men went about the store warehouse area picking up supplies, grain, tools, and a hand drill with bits. Jocko added some staples and nails for fencing to the stack.

Jocko smiled and nodded his head, agreeing with Huffman about how he felt about Annie. "Yep. She's my girl from here on out." He walked to the front counter where the growing stack of purchases waited to be boxed for the wagon ride back to the homestead.

"We don't plan to be in town again until spring, I reckon, so's I want to get everything I can buy today." He pulled out his hand-tooled elk-leather wallet to finish up their transaction. Huffman made the marks in his ledger.

"Annie won't be back this way for another couple of hours, Jocko. Let's go get us some coffee and a cinnamon roll over at the café. We got lots of work done and more to go. I need a break." Huffman turned over his sign that guarded the front door. On one side it said OPEN and on the other, I'M DRINKING COFFEE. BE RIGHT BACK.

The two men walked down the boardwalk toward the café when Jocko spotted Conley's Gun Store. He tugged at the other man's sleeve.

"Let's make a detour here. I need to get some powder and shot for my meat hunting trips." Jocko heard the bell tinkle overhead when he opened the shop door. He wasn't two steps into the building when he spotted the Winchester rifles. The temptation was too great. He lifted the repeating rifle to his right shoulder and peered down the long barrel.

"That's a real beauty. It has a tag on it for $60.00." Mr. Conley was sitting behind a counter reading the Philipsburg newspaper.

Jocko put the rifle back on the rack. "Maybe next trip, my friend. All I need today is shot, powder, matches…."

"Yeah. This old fool is hitching up with Annie Morgan. He just bought a gold band over at my place." He slugged Jocko's arm. The other man came around the counter and did the same thing. "You leaving your place near Stump Town?

"Jocko bought Annie a sewing machine today, too. He's really serious. Why, he turned down this here Winchester." He stroked the wood on the side of the rifle. "Better take a second look, Jocko."

"Naw. My trusty rifle has been with me since Civil War days. I'm not going to part company now. Besides, these new repeating rifles make too much of a clitch-clatch when you drop a shell into it to get ready to fire off a shot." Jocko accepted the good-natured ribbing from the two men.

Jocko paid for the supplies, and the three men left, after inviting Conley to join them for that now much needed cup of coffee. "I hope there's still a few rolls left by the time we get to the café," said Jocko, now suddenly very hungry.

Singer Sewing Machine

MEMPHIS DAILY APPEAL (Memphis, TN) November 10, 1861, p.2 c. 8

Sewing Machines!

Repaired, and new parts furnished, if necessary, no matter who made the Machine. We repair all kinds. We have Needles to fit Howe's, Singer's, Wilcox and Finkle's and Lyon's. Clocks repaired.

Watches repaired. Jewelry and Silverware repaired. We are giving more attention than ever to all kinds of repairs, having but little else at present to do.

# ~ 15 ~

▼

# LEAVING TOWN

"Would you look at that wagon, loaded full up?" Annie held the rope tight while Jocko made the last knot, holding the tarp tightly in place. Jocko did a great job of packing and stacking so that everything would ride as smoothly as possible on the rutted dirt road back to the homestead.

With one last look around, Jocko pulled his cabin door shut. He loaded his hunting gear, traps, fishing equipment, and tarps: things he knew would not be there long once word got out he was abandoning the shack for Annie's homestead. Even though he would still be the official owner, if another miner wanted to move in for a spell, Jocko would not stop him.

"Goodbye, shack. You served me well for many years." Jocko saluted the cabin and quickly climbed aboard the wagon seat. Annie sat still and was quiet. She sensed this moment was yet another parting in Jocko's list of partings since he'd left New Jersey as a teen. He had enlisted in the War between the States. *I must ask him about those years*, she thought.

- - - - - - -

The two days spent in Philipsburg had passed quickly. Both were a little sorry to have to leave the bright lights and warmth of friends and conversations both had had with others.

The Bucket of Blood Saloon treated them both well, and Annie enjoyed the stories Jocko told. He had mountain man stories about near death experiences, but the one story the men wanted to hear was how Fisher Jack got his new nickname, 'Jocko'.

Every time a new patron came into the bar and saw Jocko, he was asked, "Hey! Fella, what's your name?" Annie laughed as he embellished the story, until even she didn't recognize her part in the drama.

Annie had made a good trade at the mercantile store. She found most of the items on her list. She was pleased with the yarn selection. She picked dark wool for socks, and an oatmeal color yarn to make Jocko a surprise sweater for a Christmas present.

Not having to card her own wool into yarn was a luxury for Annie. She did have wool waiting for her to clean, card and spin, but that was a project for another day. Now that Jocko was her helping hand, she would be able to get to many of her set-aside projects. The sacks of wool that hung from the rafters in the old barn brought to mind an old nursery rhyme.

Feeling very flush with money from her trades made, she looked for a gift for Jocko. She was delighted to find a variety of men's hats and caps. She chose a Donegal tweed Irish cap for Jocko. He'd save it for when they came to town again, she knew, and he'd tell her she was being extravagant. But she also knew he would wear it for the rest of his life.

"I think this was a wonderful trip, Jocko. It was so helpful to have you with me to lift all the heavy sacks of feed we are takin' back for the animals.  The horses and chickens will thank you in about another two months when they are confined to the barn for days on end."

Jocko nodded his head. He needed to concentrate on driving the wagon to the outskirts of town. Coming off the hillside always made him a bit uneasy when driving a team. A stray dog, or another team of horses coming toward him on the cross street, could cause a problem for him and his driving. But, fortunately, this day, no mishaps occurred. It was early morning, still dark and cold, and not too many people were moving about. The horses were fresh and ready to pull their load home.

Bingo sat up on the wagon seat beside Annie. She put her hands into his thick, black and white, longhaired coat and was comforted by his warmth and the feeling of his beating heart.

Mouser, still the best-kept secret of the whole trip, had silently waited her turn. She had jumped into the tail end of the wagon, made a spot for herself once again on the top of a stack of blankets, and licked at her fur. She had found Philipsburg a bit more than she bargained for the first night when she unexpectedly met the town's alley cat.

"Sure glad you brought along our heavy winter coats, Annie. It feels like we might run into some weather going home."

Annie smiled. It was nice to hear Jocko say, "going home" to her. The only disturbing incident the whole trip was when they went to visit with Judge Durfee, recently elected to the office of County Attorney of Deer Lodge County. As the county attorney, it would be up to him to help Annie file new claim forms for the homestead. All she wanted to do was add Joseph Case's name to the papers in order to protect him in case she died. The Judge wasn't all that in favor of it when Annie told him the reason for her visit to his office.

"You two do know you can't legally marry each other here in Montana Territory don't you?" He spoke with true prejudice in his voice and actions. "Annie are you sure you want to do this? It's all you have from my giving you that cabin you live in."

Annie bristled but she held her tongue. She did not want to discuss the terms of how she got the cabin. It was not long after she accepted the cabin for payment of her nursing and tending to a relative of the Judge, that she applied for homestead on one hundred and sixty acres back under the shadow of Hog Back Mountain.

"Oh, yes, sir. We are aware and now duly informed by the law," said Jocko. "But that isn't going to stop us from having a hand-shake agreement." Jocko looked up and stared right at the attorney.

"You married, are you?"

"Yes, sir, I am," said Mr. Durfee.

"Well, you ever hear of "common law" marriage?" Jocko didn't wait for an answer. He reached into his pocket and pulled out the black box containing the gold band, the surprise he had purchased for Annie at the mercantile store.

"This here ring belongs to my Annie." He slipped it onto Annie's finger and, luckily, it was large enough to work its way over her gnarled ring finger.

"Well, Mr. Attorney, now I am happily married common law. I'll see to it that my name is painted right on to the mail box first thing when we get back to the homestead." He smiled. "I read that makes it legal iffen we do that. The other requirement of being together for seven years is going to fly by."

They left the attorney's office, their legal business now taken care of.

Annie kept twirling the new, shiny gold band, and couldn't help but give out a real gutsy, honest-to-goodness laugh of pure joy.

"Didn't I already tell you about the marriage laws? You jess didn't believe me, you old fool. Well, now the whole town of Philipsburg is goin' to know what we been up to." Annie moved over closer to Jocko on the wagon seat.

"Thank you, Jocko, for being my companion. One lifetime will not be long enough for us, I'm a thinkin'."

Jocko grew pensive. "Then Annie, we will just have to have another hand-shake deal about that lifetime of being together. Our spirits will remain on this homestead forever. How's that sound?"

Both Annie and Jocko became very still and silent. They listened to the beat of the horses' hooves, the rhythm matching the beats of their hearts.

- - - - - - -

A few early morning risers on their way to the local café, waved as the wagon lumbered on down the street. The mine whistle would blow in about an hour, and the bustle of the day would begin in earnest. Bess and Bob would be well on their way to their hay meadow near Rock Creek long before that sound would echo over the valley floor.

"It's too bad we couldn't get the homestead paper signed and filed this trip, Jocko. It'll be ready for our signatures in the spring when we get back to town again. I'll put the copy with my will that I keep in a coffee tin on the shelf in the barn. Remind me to show you where that is when we get home."

- - - - - - -

# Cost of Food Prices and Wages in the 1800's

1 bag of flour $1.80

¼ lb. Of tea      .38

1 qt. Milk        .56

1 lb cheap coffee .35

Sugar 3 lb. @  $1.05 lb.

4 lb.butter @ $1.60 lb.

2 lb lard .38

Dried apples  .25

Vegetables .50

Soap, starch, $1.00 ea

Pepper, salt, vinegar, $1.00 ea

2 bushels of coal $1.36

Kerosene .30

Sundries .28

Rent $4.00 per week

## Wages

The average wage earner made $16.00 a week.

Some trades only made $2.00 and some made $6.00.

There was never money left over for entertainment or clothing. In New York City, men driving the streetcars in the 1880's made $1.75 a day working 14 to 16 hours per day.

During this period of American history, children were employed, and worked 14 to 16 hours per day. They were paid in pennies.

# ~ 16 ~

▼

# ANNIE'S STORY

Something was troubling Jocko. Annie felt the tension in his body, the rigidity of his back, the way he kept looking over at her.

"Jocko, what's troublin' you, this day?"

Jocko kept his eyes on the road ahead. Daylight was casting long shadows and the scene was awesome before him. Everything was waking up. Birds flew high in the air; bugs flitted about, some in the path of the hungry hawks. It seemed to Jocko that the whole world was turning from black to vivid colors as the grasses waved their good morning to the pair on the wagon seat.

Bingo had jumped out of the wagon and was trotting alongside the horses, veering off path to chase after a rabbit, then hurrying to catch up to the team again. Nothing should be bothering Jocko, but Annie had caught him in a pensive mood.

"Annie, I'm just going to come right out with it. I am so sorry for some of the things said to you back in town by Judge Durfee, and the way you were snubbed by some of the women in the stores. I knew it happened other places but for some reason, maybe because there are no other colored women in Philipsburg, I never gave it no mind as to how you'd be treated."

Annie took her turn at staring straight ahead. *How should I answer him? The truth is always the best, and I want Jocko to know how I feel.*

"When Judge Durfee found me in Ft. Benton a few years back, he was lookin' for a woman to come over here to the cabin on the Hog Back to take care of his sick uncle. The fool drank too much and ruined his liver." Annie paused for a second.

"I hired on, thinkin', 'Why not' I ain't doin' nothin' around here'. So, I left that part of Montana Territory and the company of colored who had gathered in Ft. Benton. I struck out for Helena, then Philipsburg. The Judge, he lived part time in Virginia City at the time. He set me up in the cabin with the uncle. We got me that cot you been sleepin' on in the barn." She took a deep breath.

"Well, the old fool lived for a while and seemed to be gettin' better under my nursin' skills, but then he jess took a turn and was gone. I notified the Judge. I was to be paid for my services, but the Judge decided to give me the cabin for pay. That was okay by me. I took what he gave. Then I filed for a homestead and now I have one hundred and sixty acres with my name on the title. Ain't that somethin?"

Jocko turned his head in disbelief. "You mean you were left just that cabin? How did you manage alone with a sick man to tend?"

"It weren't for very long, Jocko. And I didn't try to fix up things. I jess went about my daily chores. I milked Bossie, and I had Bess and Bob to tend to. And you know what? I found a real fondness for fishin'. Yes, sir. When things got to me, I'd go fishin." Annie laughed. "We sure did eat a lot of fish back then. I had my garden, although not nearly the size it is today. That came later." Again, Annie laughed.

"Fishin' you out of Rock Creek was a godsend, my friend. You'll be the one to help me do the improvements needed to keep the place. I want to add another one hundred and sixty acres, too."

Intrigued now, Jocko wanted to know more. He wanted to know about her time spent before the Civil War, and before coming into Montana Territory.

"Tell me more, Annie. Will you? How did you get into Montana Territory?"

Annie squirmed. "I need a drink of water first, Jocko. Why don't you pull over at Willow creek? It's jess around the bend, and you can splash the team through it. That's about eleven miles out of town and a good shady spot for the horses to rest a bit. We can stop for a light meal and have some leg-stretching time. I'll gather my thoughts about goin' back so far into my past. I can guarantee you it's nothin' special."

She whistled for Bingo to stop chasing butterflies and to keep up with the team. "You're goin' to be one tired out dog by noon, Bingo. Get on over here with us, now. Come on."

With a practiced hand, Jocko took the horses through the small creekbed and pulled up beneath the most beautiful tree he'd seen in several days. The leaves had turned since they had been here only a couple of days ago, and yet they were still strongly clinging to the branches. No wind had been through, apparently, although Jocko's left knee was beginning to ache;

that was his bodily warning that the weather was about to abruptly change.

Annie took her time spreading out a lunch of water, bread that she tore into chunks, jelly, and some oranges she had purchased from the grocery store. A nice breeze stirred underneath the golden umbrella of leaves, and Annie and Jocko both stretched their spines at the same time.

"Come, Jocko. Sit." Annie patted the tarp she had spread for them to sit or lay upon for a little while. He dropped to his knees and then squatted back onto his boot heels. He reached for a chunk of bread, took the cup of water and ate.

"So, you's curious about Annie? Well, first off, I was born into slavery 'cause my mama was a slave. John Morgan owned her, and he had a plantation. My mama was an inside servant. She waited hand and foot on the mastah's wife, and she taught me to do the same. No field hand slave for her baby girl, no suh." Annie stroked the top of her leg a bit, and then continued.

"By the time I was seven I was working in the garden helpin' out Cook." Annie stopped for a minute with a quizzical look on her face. "I never did know her name. She was jess 'Cook'. She took me under her wing and taught me about cookin' good; how to use herbs and spices for the Mastah's taste. She taught me about doctorin' and how herbs healed things gone wrong." Annie drank deeply from her cup of water. Jocko put his hand out to her, but she did not take it. It was as if she had gone into a deep, dark place and had to work her way back out of it.

"I learned to read and write, and to polish silver, and sweep and clean.

By the time I was a young woman, I was birthin' babies for the field hands' women in trouble down in the shacks they had to live in. I still can smell that unwashed stink. The overseer would send for me. He didn't want no slave dyin' and the Mastah takin' his anger out on him. So's I learn't nursin', and cookin'.

"My mama and me, we had a nice room in the cellar of the plantation mansion. My life was good. My mama kept me away from the boys on the plantation, too. 'No nonsense for my Annie,' she'd say. Annie paused, remembering mama's overprotection of her.

"Mama would switch me on my legs all the way back into our room if she caught me flirtin' with a boy." Annie paused, as if to collect her thoughts.

"Then one day the mastah, he come into the house where Mama and I was scrubbin' the pine plank floors. He was screamin' at us to get up. He wanted his clothes packed and the wagon loaded right then. He and his missus were leavin' the plantation. The field hands had set fire to the fields, and there was so much noise and fear. We didn't know what was happenin'."

Annie's voice changed, and she started talking faster. Fear crept into her eyes, and she clasped her hands to her chest.

"He grabbed my mama and took her to tend to his packin'. He had a wild man's eyes about him. He ran to the kitchen and told Cook to get food packed. I backed into a corner behind a velvet drape and shook 'til he turned on his heel and ran back outside. A groomsman had brought up the best pair of horses, a matched set of trotters, and had them hitched to a Brougham buggy. He also had two of the best farm animals hitched up to the wagon being loaded in the front yard. I saw my Mama runnin' back and forth and she looked scared, too."

Jocko stayed very quiet, fascinated by this story, and not wanting her to stop telling it.

"Mama looked for me, found me, and shouted. 'The Union soldiers are comin' to take over the plantation and mansion.'

The mistah wanted to be gone before they arrived. Cook and me…we were goin' to be left behind."

"Next' thing I was runnin' outside. Runnin' as fast as I could down the back way to the river. I knew Mama was goin' to be dragged along to tend to the missus and the mastah. Cook would be left to fend for herself. She'd be feedin' the Union soldiers and takin' care of the Union general who planned to move in within the hour. I jess knew I had to flee for my freedom."

- - - - - - -

Annie rubbed her temples and stood up. She walked around the wagon and petted Bess and Bob. She whistled for Bingo to come near again. It was then she spotted Mouser peeking out of the wagon bed.

"Well, well. Lookee' here. We got us a stowaway." She grabbed the cat by the scruff of her neck and pulled her out of the wagon. She walked over to Jocko. "Best pour her some water, Jocko." Annie stroked the unwilling cat. Bingo came over to sniff Mouser to check her out, too.

"We best be packin' up, Jocko. I'm needin' a break, anyways." Annie busied herself packing up the remains of the picnic, keeping Mouser tucked under her left arm.

Jocko replaced the bridles on the horses, and helped Annie get into the wagon. She still held on tightly to Mouser, but Bingo, not to be outdone by any cat, jumped into the wagon, then climbed over the tarp to set himself between Annie and Jocko. It meant close contact with Mouser, but he was willing to chance a paw full of claws on his nose.

"Gee, haw!" Jocko shouted out to the horses, now refreshed and ready to get on with the trip to their hay meadow. He pointed them down the rutted road towards the Hog Back.

He wanted more from Annie, but decided she'd tell him when she was ready.

Finally, Annie tossed Mouser onto the tarp behind Bingo, who was still rigidly guarding his mistress. "Relax, old dog, and leave Mouser be."

"Jocko, now my story changes a bit for the better." Annie looked at him to see his face and the reaction she expected he would have. She hoped it wouldn't send him on down the road in the morning, but she had to tell him all.

"I am going to tell you the rest of my story, but only this onest time, so listen up."

Jocko smiled at that. "Annie. Your story is safe with me. I doubt it can be any more sorry than mine after my time in the Civil War. I'll tell you about it sometime, too. But this is your time, so I'm listening."

"I ran and ran, until I couldn't run no more. I wasn't goin' to be no slave for Union soldiers, let me tell you, no way. I hid in the bushes when I heard them comin'. They sure was noisy with all the wagons and cannons, and horses and more soldiers than I'd ever seen in my life walking down the road headed for the plantation. For a moment I wondered if I should turn back to help Cook. But I knew I wouldn't do it. I didn't feel bad either, when I kept goin' north. I was headin' for freedom."

Bingo barked and wanted off the wagon seat now that his guarding session had ended.

"Whoa, Bess. Whoa, Bob, let's get ole Bingo to the ground."

Bingo jumped down easily, and ran off ahead of the trail.

"The energy a dog has is so curious a thing, isn't it, Annie?"

Annie nodded. She was eager to continue now that she was into the story.

"Night came on me, Jocko. I met up with some other colored folks, and we ran together on into the night. We came up on a soldiers' camp and smelled stew and coffee. Some guards were walking back and forth, but others were sleepin' on the job. We slipped by them so easy. We got some loaves of bread offen a table near the edge of the camp. Some of us made it back out, but I didn't. A big Union soldier, watchin' me, grabbed me by the arm and hung on so tight I thought he'd break it.

"Whatcha think you be doin'?" he shouted at me. I was so scared I couldn't speak nothin'."

"Next thing I know, I'm standin in front of a Union general: a man with long, yellow hair and blue eyes. He had bars and stars on his uniform." Annie looked over at Jocko. He stared straight ahead, watching the road.

"The general looked me over real good. Then he said, 'Release her, soldier. If she is hungry get her some food.' I took a breath and stood very still in front of this man."

"What can I do for you, Missie?" he asked ever so polite.

"I's freedom runnin', suh. Do you need a cook? I can cook real good.  I'm strong and heal with herbs, too. I could help you here in your camp and tend to your wounded men."

"'Aren't you the bold one?'" said the yellow haired general. "'Do you know who I am?'" he asked me."

"No suh, I said. 'Just that you's a Union side soldier.'"

The yellow-haired general tipped back his head and roared with laughter.

"'Missie,' he said, 'I am General George Armstrong Custer. Fate has brought you to this camp, as I am in need of a good, strong cook who can heal my men. You want the job, you got the job. Now, go clean up. You look like a runaway slave and a ragamuffin to me.'"

I had nothing to change into, no supplies and no food. I jess looked up at that general and I said:

"'Suh. May I scrounge for some things to wear? A pair of britches and a shirt is all I's needin'.'"

General Custer clapped his hands, and an army aid came to his side. He barked out an order.

"'Bring this here one a pair of britches and a shirt, and bring me a bottle of whiskey. The good stuff, not that rotgut in the barrels.'"

"'Yes, sir.'" The soldier saluted the general, turned on his heels and disappeared, only to return in short order with the needed clothes. He held up a bottle of whiskey and handed it to the general, who immediately tore out the cork with his teeth and took a deep swig from the bottle itself.

"So, Jocko. I started workin' that very night for the Union General. Happy I was too, 'cept I missed my mama somethin' fierce. I didn' cry out for her, not even onest, and the days turned into months. Those months turned into years.

"General Custer and I got along 'splendidly" he told me after a few weeks of eatin' my cookin'. I was his personal cook by then, and had supplies brought to me first when the soldiers would rob a chicken house, or a plantation garden that escaped bein' burned out by the plantation owners."

Annie's throat hurt. She had not talked this much at one time in her whole life. Yet a clean feeling was spilling across her body and heart. It was good to get the story out of her. And, to hear herself tell it so pure and honest, with nothing left secret. Jocko was her friend, and he would keep it between them.

"It's going to get dark on us early Annie. I'm sure glad we are on the home side of this trip." Jocko grew pensive and silent as he decided to give Annie a break from her telling. He started singing in a clear, Irish voice, a song they both recognized, and for different reasons. Annie recognized the

Garry Owen from living amongst Custer and his men. Jocko knew the song because he had marched with Custer, and with General Sherman to the sea.

Could it be that Annie was in that camp with me? If so, she saw some horrible fighting and horrific death. Hmmm. I don't think I want to know if Annie was one of the coloreds who marched right along with the whole troop. There were several colored servants who had to take care of Elizabeth Custer too, after she joined her husband at Ft. Leavenworth and then traveled with us into the Dakotas.

Jocko just wanted to shut this all out of his mind. Singing turned to Irish drinking songs, and a happier sound floated around the horses' ears as they continued the long trek home.

Annie looked about her. "We've only got about five more miles, Jocko. That's the marker over there by that fence post."

Mouser

# ~ 17 ~

▼

# HOME AT LAST

As the wagon neared the homestead line, Charlie pricked up his ears. He galloped to the fence and whinnied. Bess and Bob both whinnied their greetings back. Bingo had already ducked beneath the barbed wire fence and taken a short cut to the yard.

"Hey! Charlie. We're back!" shouted out Jocko.

Annie's infectious laugh sounded deep and robust. Only when she was content did she do so, and tonight, in the dark, knowing she was nearing her own piece of property, Annie was joyous. She had a beautiful band of gold on her finger for the first time in her life. Her future path would now have someone to walk on it with her.

Annie jumped stiffly from the wagon seat. "I'll get the gate." She swung the piece of fence open wide, and held it back until the horses and wagon lumbered on through. Jocko pulled up near the barn and set the brake.

"Hello, Charlie, I'll be right over with a sugar lump for you, old man. Did you think I'd gone off and left you?" He walked over to the fence and took a sugar lump out of his vest pocket. Charlie nickered a low, warm sound, and reached for the treat. All was well on the Morgan-Case Homestead. Jocko patted the horse on his neck and forelock before he turned back to the work waiting for him.

"Annie, iffen you'd go in and make coffee, I'll start unloading the perishable supplies."

"I'm already there, Jocko. Ones't I get the fire goin' in the stove, you'll see smoke comin' from the chimney…and then we'll know we're home for sure."

It took Jocko a while in the dark to pull off the ropes holding the tarps, but he managed to free the items that should not get wet should a storm come up. He didn't want the bedding and pillows, or the clothes and boots to get damaged. Everything they had purchased was a necessity, and he would not take a chance on losing it now that they were back home.

Annie, with a cup of steaming hot coffee for Jocko, made her way to him. He took the cup as Annie walked on by on her way to open the barn doors.

"Why don't you put the wagon into the barn for tonight? We can unpack in the daylight." She helped Jocko with the heavy canvas tarps and rolled up ropes. These she looped over hooks in the interior of the barn.

Jocko liked that idea of backing the wagon up out of the weather, and he positioned the team to back the wagon into the barn for the night. He then unhooked the team, removed their harness and hung it on hooks.

He scooped up some buckets of oats for the three horses. The latch screeched as he opened the gate to the hay meadow, and he pumped fresh water into the tub. The calf and cow made soft lowing sounds but stayed at the end of the meadow.

"Annie, I am so tired. It is just nice to be home."

What Jocko failed to notice in the darkness was the pair of yellow eyes watching at a safe distance in the underbrush. Glowing yellow eyes meant only one thing. The mountain lion had returned, but there would be no chicken for his dinner this night. The yellow eyes blinked and disappeared into the blackness of the night.

"Bingo! What are you barking at? There's nothing out there for you to chase off tonight. Come inside and have some dinner with us."

Mouser had immediately jumped out of the wagon to her hiding place inside the old barn, crawling through the hole she had dug near the edge of the foundation on the far side of the building. She would be safe and secure from the yellow eyes that had failed to spot her as she made the dash to her nest.

All was well with everyone. The sales of their wares had gone well. Annie had made good bargains for many of the items on her list. Now the trip to Philipsburg, her only vacation for months to come, was a happy memory.

"G'night, Jocko." Annie sat in her rocking chair in the dark. She heard snoring, deep and even, that told her Jocko was already out for the night. Wearily, she stood, stretched and blew out the lantern. In the dark, she stripped off her travel clothes, tossing them over the back of the rocker. She walked to the edge of the bed, touched his head tenderly, and was pleased to see her gold band flash a gleam of light. "See you in the mornin'."

# Coffee Recipes
## For the Frugal Housewife 1833 - 1860

### Alternatives for the coffee bean.

Acorns, barley, beans, beets, bran, chestnuts, corn meal, cotton seeds, dandelion, okra seeds, sweet potatoes, peas, peanuts, persimmons, rice, rye sorghum molasses, sugar cane seeds, watermelon seeds, wheat berries.
Parch, dry, brown roasted to make ersatz coffee.

### Recipes

Sweet potato coffee: Pare potatoes, cut into small bits, dry and parch, add a little butter before taking from the oven to grind.

Tubers like carrots or yams: Cut into small pieces, dried, toast and grind up.

A 'receipt' for coffee from ripe acorns: wash them in the shell, parch until they open, remove the acorns and roast with a little bacon fat.

Dandelion coffee: Cut roots into small pieces, roast in the oven until brown and crisp, and then grind.
Peanut coffee: Cup of peanuts, roast all to a rich coffee brown; grind and make as for Postum.

A better taste for habitual coffee drinkers, use one-third real coffee to make the above recipes more acceptable.

Taken from the Wilmington Daily Journal, 3 October 1861.

# ~ 18 ~

# ANNIE'S MEMORIES

Annie's feet had barely hit the floor when she heard the rooster crowing in the yard. Dressing in her work clothes, Annie shook Jocko's shoulder.

"Time to get these ol' bones a movin', Jocko. Mornin' comes mighty early on the Hog Back."

Jocko groaned, and turned over on the mattress to face Annie.

"Annie, we did it. I am a happy man this morning, and as far as I am concerned, you are my wedded wife forever, not just for the rest of our lives." Annie leaned over and gave him a kiss smack on the lips.

"Get up, I said." She then playfully pushed on his shoulder, trying to get him out of bed. "We have a wagon to unload, and the weather might not be so nice in a little while. The wind is up already. I can hear it liftin' the loose roofin' on the front side of the cabin."

"So, the honeymoon's over?" Jocko saw the pillow come sailing towards his head. "Okay. Let's start our first day of wedded bliss. You call it, Annie."

"I call it? Then you get up, and let's get busy. I want to see all the things I bought in town." Sheepishly, she added, "I kind of went overboard on a few things. But, I really did make out like a bandit selling all the eggs and vegetables I had. Mr. Shodair bought them all, so's I didn't have to travel to the other grocery stores, or to the mine cooks." She smiled, remembering the conversation between the store manager and herself.

"He said I beat the other gardeners in with my fresh produce, and it all looked so nice and clean. Why, even the potatoes were brushed and in sacks, onions on strings for hangin'. He couldn't refuse to take them."

"I noticed all your vegetables in the bins in the windows, when we drove by there yesterday morning on our way out of town." Jocko spoke with pride in his voice as he continued to praise Annie for all her hard work.

"Why, you old fool, you worked jess as hard as I did gettin' it all ready." Annie had moved to the kitchen, and started making their breakfast.

Jocko went out to tend to the animals. He let the cabin door slam shut behind him, and he started humming a pub song as he walked to the barn.

*First thing I better do is milk old Bossie. That calf isn't going to like me being back, but Annie is going to need milk today, and I want some cream for my coffee.* He found the three-legged wooden milk stool, and a clean bucket to put some oats into for the cow. He took down a milk pail hanging on a hook on the inside of the stall.

"Hoa there, Bossie. How's about you and me getting down to business here. Yes, ma'am, you sure do look swollen up and ready to give me some good milk."

Jocko heard a soft meow.

"Well, good morning, Miss Mouser. I bet you'd like some nice, warm milk, too." Jocko sprayed one teat toward the cat. Mouser, skilled at this game, jumped up on her hind legs, and opened her mouth to catch the stream of milk. Over and over, Jocko played with Mouser, until she ran off into her hiding place.

The milking done, Jocko turned Bossie and the calf out into the meadow. Even though they were late getting in the night before, Jocko had chased her out of the meadow, and into the barn for the night. He knew he'd be milking her earlier than usual, and he didn't want to walk through the tall, damp grasses covered with morning dew. His plan was a success, and he smiled at his cleverness.

"Breakfast is on the table," yelled out Annie, cupping her mouth with her hands to make sure Jocko heard her. "Come and get it while it's hot."

Before going back inside, to the warmth, and comfort, and smells of a wonderful breakfast, Jocko walked over to check on the chickens. He opened the latch, and let the birds fly free into the yard. They were after insects as soon as they returned to the earth. The new chicken coop had held up well. Jocko would check for any signs of wild animals hanging around the coop later in the morning. Now he wanted to eat some food himself.

Jocko brought the milk in and set it on the table top. He wolfed down the home-cooked meal and belched his approval. Annie, so happy to have Jocko with her, was going to see to it that he got good, nourishing meals, the kind she had cooked for General Custer back in Ft. Leavenworth, and at the Battle of the Little Big Horn.

*Sometime I'll have to finish up my story about workin' for the general and his missus,* thought Annie.

But, all of that was soon forgotten, as Jocko carried in box after box from the wagon to the cabin floor. *Where will we store all of this? My goodness, I did get a bit carried away, but I had to consider Jocko livin' here now, too.*

It didn't take Annie too long to sort and decide what to keep in the house, what to take to the barn, and what to put in the vegetable root cellar across the roadway in the side of the mountain. She had a great dugout over there, where the temperature stayed around 50 degrees summer and winter.

Jocko patiently carried the boxes to their designated new locations. He stopped on occasion to talk to Charlie at the fence line when he had something for the barn. Bingo jumped around his legs, demanding to be petted, and Jocko had some dried bread chunks in his pocket for the dog to chase after and eat.

Annie waited until he was out of the cabin. *Oh, Jocko, this is goin' to be a fine Christmas this year for both of us. I think this Irish cap will look jess right on you.* She quickly closed the lid on the small box, and put it inside a larger one that held sewing supplies.

Annie, while in Daniel Stewart and Company's mercantile store, found several yards of colorful calico. She looked over her selections, and was very pleased with her choices. She had one very bright pattern with paisley swirls in blues and greens and dotted purples. Another cloth remnant was a heavy cotton twill to make herself a work skirt that would not tear easily when she worked around the farm. The third yardage was bright red. She had enough to make a blouse to wear on Christmas day with a black, wool, full-length skirt she kept in her trunk. *Now that Jocko is here, I will have to dress nicer for him,* she told herself as the reason for being so extravagant.

Usually Annie did not splurge on goods for herself, but this time was different. She had a need for the materials, and she convinced herself, she needed the hair combs, too. Annie stuck the two matching amber combs into her thick black, kinky hair. They were large and held her hair back on the sides rather stylishly. Annie peeked at her self in the small glass mirror that hung over the washbasin stand.

"Oh! My! Would you look at me?"

"I'm looking, my girl."

Annie whirled around to face Jocko. She had not heard him come in.

She reached up to pull out the combs.

"Leave them in, for a little while, Annie. Let's enjoy the things you bought. This way I get to see all of your purchases." Annie complied to his wishes and hummed a happy tune as she continued sorting through the stuff.

- - - - - - -

The store owner had purchased all of the knitted scarves, mittens, gloves, wool socks, for men, women and children. He also wanted the crocheted hats and vests that Annie had made over the long winter of the year past. He knew every one of the items would be sold within a few weeks for Christmas gifts.

Annie traded for more quality yarns that had just come by railroad from Drummond that very weekend. The colorful selection, and the strands against Annie's harsh and gnarled hands, felt so tantalizing that she had to make herself stop selecting.    She wanted enough of the soft wool for a nice sweater for Jocko.    She had chosen an Irish oatmeal color, knowing she would need many of the skeins to complete the project.

Next, she went to look at buttons. She was surprised at their expense. *My goodness, I am not paying a penny each for buttons. Jocko will have to saw me some deer antler slices for me to use as buttons. He can cut me some bush branches, too. They make unusual buttons.*

The clerk had helped Annie load all of her boxes full of precious surprises and household items. She purchased one bar of French milled soap. It was an extravagance, but she could not pass it up. She did not want or need perfumes, but now that Jocko was going to be around, she wanted to be more feminine.

- - - - - - -

By mid-afternoon, Annie had sorted her purchases, and everything was in its designated place. She put the flour, salt, sugar, and soda…fragile staples used in baking…into the small room off the kitchen. The roof was solid there and there was no window, so Annie never worried about rain coming in, and ruining her flour and other supplies. The lamp oil was placed on the bottom shelf.

On a whim, she had purchased raisins, walnuts, candied fruits, cinnamon sticks, and roots, like ginger and nutmeg. She had even purchased a box of chocolate powder, wanting to bake special treats.

With a sigh, Annie hid the surprises for Jocko under the bed, back against the wall, where shoes, slippers, or the circular rag rug would not bump into it, giving it away.

# ~ 19 ~

▼

# WINTER COMES SOFTLY

"Would you look at that?" Annie was standing barefooted on the wooden plank floor. She could see her breath, but she didn't pay any attention to it. Her focus was on the windowpanes.

"Jack Frost came to visit us last night." Like a child wrapped in the spirit of wonder, Annie stared at the intricate designs fastened to the inside of the window squares.

"It looks like we had us a magic fairy wand strike the cabin during the wee morning hours."

Jocko, also awake now, joined in her fantasy. "If only you could crochet doilies to  capture that lacy design," he paused to stare at the lovely scene.

"Brr. It's cold in here." Jocko had jumped out of bed, still wearing his nightcap and flannel nightshirt that trailed behind him.

"Just the sight of you in that get-up makes me laugh every time," said Annie as she joined him in the job of getting the stove started up again.

Sometime during the night the fire had gone out. This rarely happened, as Jocko made a point of stoking the wood before bedtime. This cold stove was a great indicator that the temperature had dropped severely in the early morning hours.

"I'll bet it's colder than…"

"Jocko! Don't you blaspheme in here," cut in Annie before he could finish his sentence. "Jess get a fire goin'. I'm gettin' back under the covers until you do." Annie walked back to the bed and true to her word, she climbed back into it, pulling the heavy wool blankets over her.

A beautiful hand made star quilt hung over a wooden holder at the foot of the bed. Annie, every night, carefully folded the quilt and placed it onto the wooden stand Jocko had made for her a few weeks back. The work Annie had put into the quilt was laborious, every stitch properly placed until the points on the star were perfect. The quilt was the brightest item in the cabin and it was strictly for decoration, at least for now, or until she managed to work on another piece this coming winter. Finding scraps of material to put into a quilt took the most of her patience, since Annie used every piece of cloth she had until it was a rag.

Occasionally, when she met with her friends in Philipsburg, they would give her their old dresses, as they knew she liked to quilt. Annie always thanked the ladies for their contributions to her craft. And when she returned home, she put the castoffs into a ragbag until she could cut the material into the necessary squares or triangles.

Annie also made rag rugs that sold very well at the general mercantile stores in town. The ladies would gather around, and point and laugh, when they would spot a piece of their old cotton dress, now made into a colorful round rag rug. Many a time Annie thought it was because of that recognized piece of cloth that resulted in a sale for her.

Jocko put on his clothes and his heavy jacket and boots to check on the storm that had come softly during the night. When he opened the door a blast of cold air filled the interior of the cabin, but Jocko could not believe his eyes.

Snow completely filled the doorframe. They were snowed in.

'Annie! Quick! Come, look-see. Have you got a shovel in your pantry?"

Arm-in-arm they stared at the door. "Why I've never seen the likes.

Jocko, what are *you* going to do?" She laughed. "We can't go out the window either. Look at that!"

"Well, little lady. Start digging." Then Jocko thought a minute. "I'll use the ashes shovel to get a start on this… this…" All he could do was point toward the door. Now Jocko was laughing so hard. "I really have to use the outhouse, Annie."

Jocko made a cut through the drift, put on his heavy jacket, and went in search of the chickens. He packed them into a crate he had left by the chicken coop, and brought them into the house to warm up. Then he went to the barn to check on the horses and Bossie and her calf. They were warm inside the barn.

Thankfully, the door faced towards the cabin and opposite the direction of the wind that swirled in the snow, so digging the barn door open was not the chore Jocko expected to face. He found a large garden shovel leaning up against the side of the barn.

Bingo jumped into Jocko's tracks, so he would not get buried in the four feet of snow that had fallen in the meadow flat.

*It's only November and look at this*, thought Jocko. *It is going to be long, busy winter.*

Jocko looked at the cabin's roof, and shook his head in disbelief. "Annie! Come see." He shouted to her to come outside. "It's a wonder we are still breathing." He waited for Annie to put on her heavy work jacket to join him in the yard. "Look at that buried stove pipe. No wonder the fire went out."

Jocko went into the barn and found a handmade wooden ladder. He leaned it against the cabin wall. He took the large yard shovel with him as he stepped out on to the roof. He cleared the pipe.

"Now, Annie, let's get some fire in that stove. I need a cup of coffee." Jocko shook his whole body before climbing back down the wooden ladder. "After breakfast, I'll come back and finish clearing off the snow on the roof. "Annie? How did you ever manage out here by yourself?" Jocko just shook his head at the wonder of it all.

By the time breakfast was over, the sun was shining bright. Annie and Jocko wandered outside together to stare at the work of art right in their front yard. The pine trees sparkled with diamonds glistening on top of the weighted-down branches. The hay mounds cast long shadows across the meadow snows, unbroken as yet by any animal tracks.

"Annie, this is the Master's work of art right out our window. Look at how it makes rainbows in the snow, like Christmas tree ornaments. What a treat for sore eyes." Jocko could only stand and stare at the beautiful scene Nature had placed before them. "Look! There goes a jackrabbit hopping through the drifts." Jocko was like a child standing there so engrossed in the tracks left behind the rabbit. Some magpies swarmed out of the middle of a pine tree, sending shadows across the sparkling snow. Everything was moving once again, as the temperature had risen to above zero. All of God's creatures, man and beast, at first startled to have been caught by the early winter storm, breathed in the clear, crisp air. A patch of blue sky greeted Jocko's eyes.

"Now I see what you meant when you talked about the snow that falls by Christmas back in these mountains. When you kept telling me to make the pitch of the roof steep, I didn't understand the need. I surely do now. We better stay healthy, cause we won't be going to town very soon."

"Why do you think I have a sled? We got caught sleepin' and should've felt the storm comin'." She put her hands on her hips, a gesture she used when concerned.

"We've got some work to do. The cabin roof needs sweepin'. That snow weighs a ton.  We don't need the roof cavin' in on us."

They made their way to the woodpile, and Jocko loaded up Annie's arms with chopped wood. "Let's get a stack of wood up near the door, first thing. We are going to be needing lots of it." After repeated trips to get the wood stacked neatly in place, Annie had a good path worn between the woodpile and the cabin.

She worked on a path between the outhouse and the barn, calling softly to the animals, snug inside the barn. "Do you want to come out into the yard? Come on, come on. The door's open." But the animals stayed inside the warm barn.

Annie walked to the pump handle on the well in the yard, and pumped a few times to see if the water was frozen deep in the well. Luckily, it ran freely. She hoped the one in the meadow that watered the livestock would be as generous. The animals would need fresh water and feed every day, now that the ground was covered with snow.

"Whoever was it that said life was easier, and we could be lazy in the wintertime?"

"Somebody who never lived on the Hog Back," answered Jocko.

- - - - - - -

It only took Jocko a few minutes to warm up back inside the cabin. He was trying very hard to remember something.

"Annie! It's Christmas Day!" He walked over to Annie and gave her a big bear hug. Then he started singing Jingle Bells. He motioned to Annie to join in.

*Dashing through the snow. O're the fields we go, in a one horse open sleigh.*

"Let's do it. Let's go dashing through the snow. Right after breakfast, let's hitch up Bob and Bess and go for a sleigh ride. What's you say, my girl? Huh? Let's go and have us some fun in all this fluffy white stuff."

Annie grabbed Jocko's hands and started dancing him around the room.

"Yes! Yes…what fun!" She looked out the window at the sparkling diamonds scattered over the snow where the sun bedazzled the fields. "Yes, let's get ready and go. Let's be kids. Maybe Santa will find us while we're out playin'."

She hurriedly toasted some bread, set out butter and strawberry jam, poured some coffee and without skipping a beat, gave Jocko five minutes to get ready to go out the door and hitch up the sled to the team.

Jocko loved to see Annie so happy. Today was the day she would get her sewing machine, too. When they returned from the sleigh ride, he'd have her help him move that big bulky wrapped-up box in the barn, then watch her take off the tarp. He wished he had thought to get some red ribbon to put on top of it, but he guessed it would be okay just the way it was.

"Waiting for a Chinook" or the Last of Five Thousand

The winter of 1886 proved to be extremely cold and harsh
all over the Montana Territory. Charles M. Russell, a
cowboy who liked to sculpt and paint, and who ranched
near the Lewistown area, painted a watercolor of a starving
steer. There is a wolf waiting off to the side. He titled
it, Waiting for a Chinook ---The Last of the 5000.  He
mailed it to the ranch owner who lived away from the
ranch.  Thousands of cattle died in just a few days, putting
many ranchers out of business.  One of those ranchers was
Theodore Roosevelt.

Print used with permission from The Montana
Stockgrowers Association, Helena, Montana.

# ~ 20 ~

▼

# CHRISTMAS DAY

Over the past several weeks, Annie had secretly been knitting Jocko a beautiful sweater, done in an Irish design with fancy knots in it. Last September, she had asked Jocko to saw her some deer horns into slices and to drill two holes for buttons. She was very pleased with the way the yarn, oatmeal color, worked up for her. She spent time in the afternoons to work on her knitting projects. Even though many times Jocko had been in the room, it never dawned on him that Annie was working on a sweater for him. He watched her make a pair of warm knitted mittens in one afternoon, and he complimented her on her skills.

"How your fingers fly when you are knitting. And the end results, whether it is socks or a scarf, you put so much care into your craftsmanship," he said.

Annie had hidden the bulky sweater in a box, wrapped in brown paper and tied with string. She used colored chalks to draw a Christmas tree, some bells, and other ornament designs on the package. It gave the box a festive look.

While Jocko scurried out to the barn to get the horses ready for the sleigh ride, Annie pulled out the bed. She picked up the box with the Donegal tweed cap for Jocko. She giggled, and started singing *Jingle Bells* all over again.

Over the past several days, Annie had been busy making Christmas cookies and candies, hiding them from Jocko. Whenever he'd come into the house, he would smell cinnamon, or ginger, but there was never any sign of baking going on. Once, he did catch her pulling out gingerbread men cookies, but she'd slapped his hand away. "Don't you go eatin' any of them cookies. They are for the Meyers children," she had told him. *Well, today's the day to get the cookies to the Meyers ranch*, she thought.

Annie had a prime ham that she had soaked in apple cider for several days. It was an old southern recipe. She slid the covered pan into the oven so it could start baking while they went outside.

The cabin door burst open. There stood Jocko covered with snow. He had even put snow on his beard to make him look like Santa Clause.

"Come on, Annie. Get your warm clothes on. The team is ready to go. They are prancing around out there. Charlie wants to tag along too, so I got him tied to the back of the sled." Jocko waved his oversized leather mitten at Annie.

"I'm comin…Here I come…where's my scarf? Oh, okay. Let's go." Annie slammed the cabin door a bit hard and stepped off the porch, only to have Jocko grab her by the arm and pull her into the yard.

"What?" Asked Annie.

Jocko could only point to the cabin roof. The snow was coming off in one large, heavy layer. Once again, the cabin door was snowed in.

"Ah, it can wait. Let's go for our sleigh ride." Jocko looked at the huge basket Annie held really tight. It was loaded with breads and cookies and an applesauce cake. "Looks like we're headed for the Meyers ranch?" asked Jocko.

Annie laughed her happy laugh. "Jocko, let's go say 'howdy' to our only neighbors this wonderful Christmas Day. I am so happy to have you here by my side. It has been several years since I have had company on Christmas Day. I love you with all my heart and I thank you for being in my life." With that, Annie sighed. "Come on, you old fool. Time's a wastin'.'"

As was their routine, Annie opened the large gate, and Jocko drove the team and sled through. He waited for her to catch up. Annie nimbly jumped onto the sleigh.

The team broke through the heavy snow, and soon a rhythm kept time to the two people singing every Christmas song they could think of. Annie held back singing *Silent Night* as she wanted to save that song for when they were snug once again in their cabin. She planned to toast each other with a glass of homemade plum wine. It was at that time that she planned to give Jocko his gifts.

Annie had not been this excited about Christmas for many years. Neither had Jocko given it much thought over the years.

"You know, Annie, we don't get to attend church living way out here, but by golly, I feel like this is a church day for us right now." Jocko took a breath and exhaled, watching the white steam flow from his mouth. "I'm so thankful we are together, Annie." He looked so serious, Annie was afraid he was going to cry.

"Don't you dare get a tear in your eye now. It will freeze on your face." But, she tenderly reached over and patted Jocko on the arm. "You know I feel the same way, old friend." They both got lost in their own memories of Christmas's past, and Jocko, as if on queue, started singing *God Rest Ye Merry Gentlemen, Let nothing you dismay, remember Christ, our Savior, was born on Christmas day.*

- - - - - - -

Even though Annie had warmed up several flat river stones in the stove oven to put in the bottom of the sled to help keep their feet warm, the invigorating air soon lost its charm. Cold seeped into their bones. The Meyers ranch was a welcomed sight. They turned off the main lane, and the team lumbered on up to the house yard gate.

Annie jumped off of the sled and grabbed the hand-woven basket with both hands. "My, I really did fill this up with baked goods. I hope they drink homemade wine, too." She waited for Jocko who was tying the horses to the fence. They would not have moved, but he didn't want to chance anything unpleasant happening today.

The Meyers ranch house door flew open, and Annie saw Mrs. Meyers standing in the warmth and light of the kitchen.

"Annie! Jocko! What a pleasant surprise. Merry Christmas to you two. Come in, come in this house." She motioned to them to hurry inside, into the cheery warmth.

"Merry Christmas to all of you," said Annie as Jocko took the heavy basket from her and handed it to Mrs. Meyers. "We decided to enjoy this beautiful snow filled day and come for a sleigh ride. I hope it is not intruding on your festivities with the children?"

"Oh my no. The children have been up since early light waiting for Santa. He brought them wonderful gifts and they are off playing with their new toys. I wouldn't be surprised to find them napping, actually."

"Well, I baked them some gingerbread men." Annie smiled at the other woman. "There are some cakes for your supper tonight, too."

Mrs. Meyers took their coats. She called for her husband, Jack, to join them, and he came from the parlor where he had been taking a snooze in the overstuffed leather chair.

"Glad to see you, Jocko and Annie. Come in and sit a spell. You are brave coming out on a day like today. Wasn't that snow storm something earlier this morning?" He reached for his outercoat. "We must fetch your flat stones and warm them in our oven for your return trip. It will be colder in another hour or so." With that, Jack Meyers left the house, making a very quick trip to the sled, returning with the large stones, now cold to the touch.

Jocko smiled, remembering all the snow that greeted him when he tried to open the cabin door. "I knew you got a lot of snow back up in here but I never expected it to all come in one storm," said Jocko.

Mrs. Meyers had entered the parlor carrying a tray loaded with breads, candies and cookies. She set that tray on to a small tabletop, covered in a beautiful handmade lace cloth. She then went to the kitchen for another tray that held steaming cups of coffee, each cup capped with a dollop of whipped cream. Jocko could smell Irish whiskey and he smiled, happy to be drinking an Irish coffee made the correct way. He would savor every drop. Mrs. Meyers had made it especially for him, and he appreciated her efforts.

All too soon it was time to leave. Even though Mrs. Meyers invited them to stay for supper, Annie refused the offer.

"I have a ham slow cookin' in apple cider, and we best be gettin' back to tend to it." She reached for her outer garments and stepped into her boots that both she and Jocko had taken off by the back door.

The horses whinnied when the door opened and the two came outside. Annie climbed up on the sled, after the now heated rocks had been put back in place. Mr. Meyers wrapped a buffalo hide around both Jocko and Annie's legs.

"Happy New Year to you both," Jack Meyers shouted.

Jocko snapped the reins and the horses moved together. "Happy New Year to all of you folks, too."

"That was a fun visit. Now we best get up the road and to our own supper," said Annie.

- - - - - - -

Jocko turned the horses loose outside the barn, which was not the usual routine.

He opened the barn door and looked at Annie. "Would you come inside the barn with me? I need your hands for a minute to move a box."

Annie obliged and stepped inside the barn. She heard her chickens clucking a hello, and even Mouser came over and meowed at the two of them. "What a wonderful greeting from the animals. Why, even old Bossie just gave us a moo, too."

"Here, Annie, will you grab hold of that other end of the box? It is heavy, so be careful."

Jocko was so excited, he was dancing from foot to foot, like a little boy. "Okay. Now, I've got the rope off, will you pull back the tarp for me?"

Annie reached up with her ungloved hands and pulled and tugged at the tarp. Finally, it slipped off the box and onto the barn floor. She started to fold it up, when something shiny caught her eye. She walked over to the "box" and read "Singer Sewing Machine". Her eyes flew open. Could it be? She looked at Jocko who was grinning, and looking so happy that he had been able to keep it a secret from Annie for the past several months.

"Is it really a sewing machine? I am flabbergasted. Why, I have always wanted a Singer sewin' machine. How did you know? It is so expensive. I never dreamed I'd have one of my very own." Annie couldn't stop talking. She now had the lid up, the drawers open, and the head set up on its stand. She opened the red box to see all of the loose parts: directions, belts, ruler, bobbins, needles, spools of thread, a can of oil, small scissors. "It's the deluxe model. Oh, oh. I just saw this sewing machine in the Sears, Roebuck Catalog."

Jocko came over to help her. He put his arm around Annie's shoulder and gave her a hug. "This just makes it all the more special today, Annie." He reached down and took her hand in his. "I'm glad you like it. I know you will be making quilts, and clothes, and patching my britches on it." He laughed when he looked into Annie's eyes, glistening now with tears ready to spill over. "Merry Christmas, my girl."

Annie started to laugh. "Do you know how very special it makes me feel to hear you say, 'my girl' to me? Nobody ever did my whole life but you."

Jocko grinned at Annie, but he walked over to the wall, and grabbed a shovel so he could clear the dropped snow that blocked the doorway to the cabin.

"Well, now we got to get this machine inside. Do you think we can do it over all this snow? We do have a pretty good path made from the house to the barn now, don't we?"

Annie grabbed one end and Jocko the other. "We'll get it inside. I have just the spot for it, too." *Where am I goin' to put this? Someplace special, maybe by the south wall*, she thought.

When they walked into the cabin, the aromas from the ham greeted them, and they both heard their stomachs growl.

"I'll be in after I put the horses inside the barn," said Jocko. "I'll feed the chickens and the animals, too."

Annie peeled potatoes, made coffee from her stash that she had purchased at the grocery store, brought out a jar of her canned green beans, found some rolls in the bread box that she had made the day before, and boiled a couple of eggs for a surprise to go with the ham. For dessert, she had a fresh apple pie, and sweet whipped cream to top it off.

She picked through her dishes, selecting two of her nicest plates that she saved for company. She took a crocheted lace tablecloth out of her trunk and spread it on the kitchen table. By the time Jocko came back inside, she had transformed their ordinary cabin into a sight to behold.

Red candles burned brightly on the table. Annie had slipped outside and clipped some pine boughs. These she wrapped with red ribbon bows and hung one on the cabin door. The other, held by a piece of string, adorned the window near the table setting.

She put pieces of green bough on the table in two little bowls. The ham, glazed in mustard, cloves, and other spices, sat square in the middle of the table. Steaming bowels of the mashed potatoes and green beans flanked the ham.

Jocko stepped inside and did a double take.

"Oh, Annie. This is so nice. What a wonderful Christmas Day we are having, and now a special holiday dinner." He took a deep breath and put his hand on his chest. "Aahhmm… Smell that coffee."

"Sit yourself right on down. It's all ready." Annie was so happy for this special day. She knew she would remember it always.

After Jocko had finished off two pieces of apple pie, Annie jumped up from the table and cleared off the dishes. Then she reached beneath the bedroom pillows and pulled out her two packages for Jocko.

"Here, Jocko. I made you something, and the other box came from Santa, I guess."

She couldn't help but smile as she handed him the two packages.

"Well, what have we here?" Jocko carefully unwrapped the decorated package first. Out tumbled the beautiful, handmade sweater, and Jocko jumped up from his chair.

"Annie, it's perfect. He shrugged into the sleeves and stroked his left arm, feeling the luxury of the wool. It fits me just fine." He walked over to the mirror hanging over the dresser and preened. Why I am as dressed up as a fancy opera house star." He faced Annie. I'll be the best-dressed man the next trip to Philipsburg, Annie. Why this sweater will last me forever, I am thinking."

"Here. Don't forget to open this one, too." Annie held up the smaller box.

Carefully, Jocko opened the package. He let out a whoop when he saw the Donegal tweed cap. "Where on earth did you find this? He plopped it onto his head and again walked to the mirror. "It *IS* just….*ME!*"

Annie was about to burst with happiness. She looked out the kitchen window and saw the candlelight reflecting on her face. Darkness had come early, and she knew it was time to sing one more Christmas song.

"I can't remember a better Christmas, Annie." He walked next to Annie sitting in her chair, put his hand on her shoulder, and joined in the singing with his lyrical Irish tenor voice.

*Silent night, Holy night, all is calm, all is bright....*

Ellen K Murphy

### Sleighride Jocko and Annie

▼

# MOUSER HAS KITTENS

Winters on the homestead were relentlessly long, and everything living was caught in the icy grip of freezing temperatures. A black-and-white landscape captured the stillness in the snow-laden pine branches. The white blanket of pristine snow lay as it fell over the meadow and hayfields, unbroken except for the occasional tracks made by a passing elk, or other wild animal.

Annie and Jocko moved around in silence most of the day, except to ask each other what chore to do next, or to go feed the livestock. Neither stayed outside any longer than necessary.

The five hens and one rooster spent days in the barn in a penned off area Jocko had surrounded with bunches of hay to provide some warmth for them, The hen laid a few eggs. They slept inside the cabin in a cage during the nighttime hours, when the temperature dropped below zero. Annie kept them all winter. The hens were older, and good setting hens. She would have fertilized eggs and then chicks come spring for the next summer's flock.

The only small animal not inside the cabin, although she was invited to join them, was Mouser. She had her own nest, and was cozy inside the barn. Annie made sure she had food.

One day, however, Annie heard Mouser crying, in great distress.

"Jocko. Come quick. Mouser must be caught on something."

Jocko had been working just a few feet away, his feet pumping up and down like he was pedaling a bicycle. He was spinning the grinding wheel, working on sharpening a shovel blade. He liked to work in the warmth of the barn on days when the sun tried to shine. It comforted him to be surrounded by the warmth and smells of the livestock, and he milked Bossie in the barn. Jocko spent a good deal of his waking hours working at little chores that could be done in the confines of the barn walls.

"Hurry, Jocko. We have to find her."

Jocko followed the crying sounds, and found the cat; her eyes shut tight, her body contorted in pain.

"Annie. Our little Mouser is having her first batch of kittens. She won't be too anxious to go into town with us again very soon." Jocko tried to pick up the cat to carefully put her into a wooden box.

"Let's take her into the cabin and keep her warm while she goes through this."

Mouser had other ideas. She hissed and clawed at Jocko, and made it known she wanted to be left alone.

"I guess we have to oblige, Annie. We'll keep watch from a distance, and let nature take her course."

Jocko returned to his grinding job. Annie sat on the overturned wooden box, wringing her hands. All she could do was make sure water was near by for Mouser. She filled the tipped-on-its-side box with hay, and Mouser sensed it was for her use.

*Jocko's right. She'll be better off left alone.* But still, Annie waited the night with Mouser. She didn't have a lantern, and it was definitely getting colder inside the barn as the night and darkness deepened. Annie had moved to a stack of hay, pushed it around her for warmth and to make it softer to sit on. She wrapped herself tightly in her winter cloak, woolen sweater and scarves. Not intending to, Annie fell asleep.

*What was that?* Annie jumped awake. Jocko had long since gone into the house and to bed. Something furry had brushed against Annie's leg. *Have we got rats? There. It's back again. Where is Bingo?*

Just then Annie saw two, slanted, green eyes staring at her, and she heard a soft meowing sound coming from the animal brushing against her legs.

"Mouser. You've done it. You've got babies. Good girl."

Annie reached down, and to her surprise, Mouser let her touch her and actually pick her up. "Well, Miss Cat. You need some warm milk, don't you? How many babies? I see two little naked pink balls. They don't have any hair, and their eyes are shut tight. You think your nest will be enough to keep them warm, and I guess you are right. You want to keep them barn cats jess like you?" Annie pulled her clothes tight around her body as she opened the smaller barn door. "I'll be right back."

The birth of the kittens gave Annie a sense of hope that the long winter would soon pass, and that life continued. Even in the dark depression of January, happiness and joy spread through her. *I must mark this day down in my diary.*

- - - - - - -

Rock Creek, being a fast flowing stream, did not ice completely over. Jocko had voiced his concern that they find a slow moving body of water, or a pond, where he could cut ice into squares to stack for next summer's use. He'd have to ask Annie where there was a pond nearby so that he could get the ice.

When the cowhand from the neighboring Meyers ranch knocked on the cabin door, Annie about jumped out of her skin. She had not heard him ride up, and Jocko was out in the barn where he usually spent his days. Bingo, inside the barn, was apparently sleeping, something he was doing more of this winter.

"Well, howdy do, George. Come in this house and get warm by the fireplace. I just made cinnamon rolls."

The ranchhand came in, brushing at his boots with his leather gloves.

"I smelled them clear out by the gate, Ma'am. And yes, I will sit and visit a spell, if you have a cup of coffee to go with that roll."

"Let me give a yell to Jocko. I'll be right back."

Annie was happy to have company. Visitors were special for Annie any time, but especially in the winter.

The man waited until Jocko joined him at the kitchen table before he bit into the cinnamon roll, the size of a dinner plate, and dripping with honey and butter. Annie scurried about seeing that her company was comfortable.

"I've come to invite you to an ice-cutting party. You know where the river has a big bend just outside the Meyers ranch?" George asked.

Annie nodded.

"The water pools up in there, and it is about ten inches thick right now. I've been watching it get solid and deep."

"We're going to build fires in barrels, and the kids will play with their sleds they got for Christmas from old Santy. This coming Monday morning will be the day to bring your sled and team, Annie."

"We'll be there for sure, George. Thank you for thinking of us."

"Let's get you enough ice for your icehouse that Jocko made." He looked at Annie and smiled. "Last fall, Jocko showed me how he has it all lined with hay and sawdust. It should be good and tight to keep you in ice all summer." George then looked over at Jocko. "Setting it back near the river, and in that grove of trees for shade, was a pretty smart idea."

As if he was all talked out, the cowhand jumped up. He shrugged into his canvas outer garment that hung below his knees, grabbed his fur-lined hat with earflaps, and said his goodbyes. He pulled on his leather gloves, after opening the cabin door.

"My horse won't be happy with me leaving him outside all this time, and he might decide to buck me off about four miles from home. So's I best be going. I'm not about to walk in this stuff."

He looked out into the yard where his horse was standing, head and reins down to the ground.

"We'll have us a good time Monday. Storm or no."

"Thanks for stopping by. Tell Mrs. Meyers we'll be there, and I'll bring a big elk and vegetable stew and some loaves of hard bread for lunch."

And just as swiftly as the ranch hand had appeared on their doorstep, he'd stepped off the front stoop into the silence of the white snow. The only sound was a friendly whinny from his horse, anxious to get back to the warmth of his own barn. They heard the squeak of the gate, and then quietness enveloped them once again.

"Jocko. This will be so much fun." Annie grabbed his hands and danced him around in circles in the kitchen. "I only have a day to get ready."

- - - - - - -

Annie had more than enough food and supplies packed for Jocko to load onto the sled. He had Bess and Ben hitched up, and they were ready for a good walk. Charlie was going with them, too. Jocko put a halter on Charlie's head, tying him to the edge of the tailgate. Bingo danced around.

It was as if by magic that the spell of winter's gloom lifted off their shoulders. The scales were dropped from their eyes, and color once again returned to their world.

Jocko, also caught up in the excitement of the party, found a couple of Swiss bells in the barn. Annie tied them to bright red bows that she attached to the horses' collars. The horses had to cut a path through the deep snow, and the going was slow. The jingling bells cheered up the couple.

"It feels so good to be free, Jocko. Don't you feel it, too?" Both he and Annie had energy and were not feeling the chill-to-the-bone cold.

It was a happy day to be out greeting friends, sharing stories, and getting the necessary ice. Always there was work to be done, but today they would share laughter. They would hear children shout back and forth as they tossed snowballs.

The fun would turn this wonderful winter day into a day to remember.

"Here they are. It's about time, you two. We were thinking we'd have to come and dig you out." Mrs. Meyers grabbed Annie's hands, and helped her off the sled. The stew, nestled inside the hay-lined wooden crate, smelled so good, and was still warm.

"When George said you were going to cook, Annie, I was delighted. You know we all think you are the best cook in these here parts."

Annie laughed. "Jocko sticks around cause he likes my cookin'…and I like to cook. I've had years of practice cookin' for lots of men during the war between the states." Annie looked over at Jocko. He nodded his head for her to continue.

"I cooked for General George Armstrong Custer for many years, Mrs. Meyers. He never complained a bit about my cookin." Annie dropped her eyelids and looked to the ground. She had not revealed that to anyone but Jocko, and now she felt a bit embarrassed to be talking so much. She fidgeted.

"Come on, Jocko. Let's get this food off the sled so you can join the men. That ice augur and saw you bought last trip to Philipsburg will come in mighty handy."

~ 22 ~

▼

# CUTTING ICE

Six men, working in pairs, chopped and hauled large chunks of ice from the slow-moving curve in the river. The women kept the fire barrels full of wood, made coffee, and watched the children play. Luckily, the wind was down, and the temperature comfortable.

"We've got enough ice to fill the ice house, now, George. Annie and I will be thanking you on those hot, summer afternoons when we are sipping sweet tea."

Jocko shook hands with his ice partner. "Come by any time and say 'howdy'." He looked over toward the fire barrels, and saw that Annie was waving them over. "Looks like the ladies have the food ready. I'm all for a big bowl of that elk stew."

The two men sauntered over to the makeshift table. Annie, and some of the other neighbor women, had tipped over wooden crates to make a table to hold all of the foodstuffs the six families had brought.

"Hmm. Would you look at the pies and cookies? And, look here. Who brought the oranges?" Jocko reached for an orange, and he stuck it into his inside vest pocket. "The last orange I ate was in September when we brought back some fruit." Jocko looked over at Annie and grinned.

George was standing next to Jocko and Annie. He reached for a bowl full of the hot stew. "Thank you for the lunch, Annie. Can you hand me a big spoon, too?" He turned to Jocko.

"Jocko, do you miss Stump Town? Annie's got you here workin' harder than you have your whole, miserable life." George slapped Jocko on the back, and the assembled group laughed at the joke.

"Naw. I'm happy to be where I am this winter. You folks sure do get the snow back up in here, and I'm wondering about that, but...naw...Annie takes real good care of me." Jocko took a big swig of coffee, and reached for a cookie. He put that into his pocket, along with the orange.

The women dished out the stew to all the men, then the children, and finally, themselves. "Annie, we all want this recipe," said the women as if singing in a chorus.

"Laws, ladies. It's jess elk, turnips, carrots, onions, a bit of this and a pinch of that." Annie grinned. "I jess drop in some salt, let it bubble on the back of the wood stove, and stir the juices. I add chicken broth sometimes, but mostly jess water."

One of the men spoke up. "Jocko, you sound like you might be from the East, like New York."

"Close. I was born in New Jersey. My father had a farm. I left to sign up for the Union Army during the War, and I never went back to stay." Jocko thought a minute. "In fact, I've only been back to see family maybe a couple of times. I have a niece, who lives there, but my parents are dead, and the farm has been sold to strangers. You know how that goes."

All of the members of the group nodded, or grunted a quick assent.

"What unit did you serve in during the war?"

"Well, I joined up with General Tecumseh Sherman out of New Jersey, and as my luck would have it, I marched to the sea with him." Jocko looked over at Annie. "I also spent about a month with General George Armstrong Custer, until our unit got mustered out."

Murmurs swept the little group. They all knew the Custer name.

"After the war, I headed back to New Jersey, but I couldn't settle down. I kept reliving that war and had terrible nightmares. The family just didn't understand what we young men went through. I couldn't believe I survived. Men died to the right and left of me every battle. I wandered around, doing odd jobs, no place to stay." Jocko's voice dropped to a barely audible level.

"I heard about the Fisk Overland Company, and that they were hiring men to bring the wagon trains into Montana. I went and applied for a drover's job; hired me right on the spot. I figured why not? It would be a great adventure to see the wild west, and a place for me to sleep, even if it was a different piece of ground every night.' Jocko looked around at the men. "Fisk had been a captain in the Union Army." Jocko laughed at the thought, and several of the men, lost in their own history, nodded in agreement.

"Once we got into the Dakotas, we heard about how the Indian Wars were getting really fierce. It was in Deadwood that I met up with Calamity Jane. Now there was a real story in the making in her past. She had a terrible crush on

Wild Bill Hickock and said they was lovers." Again, Jocko chuckled, thinking about the wild, woman team driver.

"Yep, she could put any one of us men under the table drinking beer and whiskey together. She called them 'boilermakers' and that they were."

"The miners in Butte drink boilermakers," said George, who had been intently listening to Jocko talk about his youth. "They put the whiskey in a shot glass, and drop it into the mug of beer."

"Have you tried it?" asked a fellow in the crowd.

"You better not have," said the bundled up woman standing by his side. She gave him a nudge with her elbow. "Back to you, Jocko."

"Well, let's see. I hunted meat for the Fisk Company. When we got into Montana Territory, I liked what I saw. Fisk wanted me to return to the east, and bring back another wagon train full of would-be farmers and settlers. I decided to quit that job, and find a cavalry outfit, and fight injuns for a while." Jocko looked over at Annie who was making herself busy at the food table.

"I was on my way to Custer's outfit to join up, when word came back that they were all killed at the Big Horn River. So, I turned old Charlie around and skeedadled it over to western Montana and Virginia City." He rubbed his forehead for a minute.

"The mines were going full blast. Yes, the miners kept spilling in to get jobs. I hired on as a meat hunter for the mine camp cooks. Kept me plenty busy, too. And, I kept the hides. Ran a trap line for beaver...that kind of stuff."

"How'd you get over here?"

"I met Judge Durfee in a bar one night in Virginia City. He told me about the Philipsburg mines, and the mountains full of game. I packed up my saddle bags and my Winchester, gave old Charlie some extra oats the next morning, and we headed out over the hills. We didn't stop until we stepped on some prickly pear cactus, near Helena." Jocko took a breath. "I had some wagon train buddies to look up in Helena, anyway, and so I had me a couple of days in the Queen City of the Rockies."

"I did the same thing," said one of the younger men who stood off by himself at the edge of the group, drinking a cup of hot coffee. "I still work the mines when the ranch work slows a bit, like now. Good thing the mines work all year round. I wonder if they need any more men to hunt meat?"

Jocko looked at the man, and gave him a name to go talk to about the meat-hunting job. "It pays good, kid. Go check it out." Jocko took Annie's hand into his gloved one when she came to stand beside him.

"I met Annie. She saved my life when I fell into Rock Creek, and almost drowned a while back. We work good together and I am a happy man. Yeah, the winter is getting mighty long, but it is amazing how much work we have to do even on the dreariest of days." He looked down into Annie's face. She was all enclosed in scarves and a fur-lined hat that covered her ears. Only a wisp or two of her black curls framed her dark face. She was smiling back at Jocko.

"You asked if I missed Stump Town? No way. I've got everything a man could want in this life right here by my side."

"Okay, Jocko. It's time to load up the boxes of stuff. Your stories can get pretty wild if we stay here much longer." Annie walked to the sled with her arms full of left over supplies.

The circled group broke apart, following Annie's lead. They called for their children and gathered up supplies. The men wandered off to hitch up their teams to their sleds loaded with the ice. The time to end this wonderful day had come.

As Jocko and Annie clicked the team into action, the sleigh bells jangled their leaving. Jocko whistled for Bingo to jump on the sled.

"Goodbye! Goodbye! See you in the spring! Stop by and visit!" shouted the women as they waved to Annie. And then Bess and Bob crossed through the timbered gate on to the dirt lane.

A comfortable silence lay between them.

"Yep. Time to go home, my girl. We've got another half a day unpacking ahead of us."

"But it was great fun, wasn't it? Annie looked into Jocko's face. "How much of your story was true?"

Jocko grinned. He lifted his chin, and started singing one of his hundreds of Irish pub songs.

# ~ 23 ~

▼

# UNEXPECTED MAIL ARRIVES

## 1889

Jocko was making the last round of cutting the hay. His eyes had been searching the heavens, and he could smell rain in the air. No matter how fast he worked, the storm would hit the meadow in a matter of minutes.

*Iffen only it don't hail. I can turn the wet, cut hay and salvage some of it for the animals to eat this winter. One more day is all I need.* Jocko took out a red handkerchief and wiped the sweat off his brow. It was then he noticed the postman dismounting from a beautiful quarter horse that stood about sixteen hands high. The horse's coat was well combed. The animal sported a long mane and tail and wore a copper brown coat.

The postman walked up to the cabin, calling out Annie's name as he walked the path. He held several letters in the air, and his excitement at being out delivering his mail made Jocko very curious.

"Hey, Henry! Over here!" Jocko gave a big wave swooping his hat in an arc over his head. He tied the reins to the team around the brake on the mowing machine, and started walking towards the postman.

At the same time, Annie had come from her garden on the opposite side of the cabin.

"Henry! What have you got for us?" Annie reached the man first. "Come inside. Have some coffee and a slice of fresh apple pie made jess this mornin'.

"Don't mind if I do sit a spell." Henry sat at the kitchen table and watched Jocko come across the meadow. "That pie looks mighty good, Annie."

"Always got pie for you, Henry. Seein' as how you always have somthin' for us in that mailbag." She pointed to the leather bag, bulging with mail.

Henry stood up when Jocko walked in to the kitchen. "Good morning, Jocko. I have some mail for the both of you today." Henry sat back down, but not before handing Annie a stack of mail, including the usual newspaper stack, and a Sears & Roebuck catalog. But, this time, there was more. Some white envelopes that looked important, dominated the top of the stack. Annie went for a sharp knife to cut the string surrounding the bundle.

"Hhmm. I wonder who is writing to us…to me…to you… Jocko?"

Annie separated the envelopes into neat stacks. She handed Jocko his stack and waited for him to open it.

Jocko spread the letters in a fan shape on the tabletop. He reached first for a letter with a government stamp on the front of the envelope. Inside was a pension check issued to Jocko for his service during the Civil War. He saw two more envelopes just like the first, and he quickly opened them and stacked the checks together.

"This money comes in mighty handy for Annie and me. We will have to get to the bank and cash them. In a few more weeks, we will be making our fall trip in to Philipsburg. I guess they will be safe in our tin can until then?"

The next envelope that Jocko picked up caused him to pause a minute. He read the return address written in perfect penmanship in the upper left hand corner. He noted the New Jersey address.

"Why this is from my niece, Eliza Case." Jocko was silent as he read the

letter. Then he repeated the words out loud for Annie and Henry to hear. "She wants to know how I am doing. She wants me to come visit her this fall."

Jocko took a sip of the coffee Annie had set in front of him before he

continued. "Now, wouldn't that be something, Annie? Would you want to take that trip back East?"

Annie took a minute before answering, but, when she did, she was firm.

"No, Jocko. I wouldn't want to go. But iffen you do, we can make some arrangements for you. You'd need at least a month." Annie looked at Jocko.

"Now wouldn't be the time for me to go, Annie. We got winter to get ready for." He put the letter back into its carefully opened envelope. "Naw. I don't think there is any time this fall for me to take a trip."

Annie smiled at Jocko, forgetting Henry was still sitting in the room.

"Iffen you want to go, Jocko, you can." She folded her hands in her lap and dropped her eyelids.

"Aw, Annie. You know I'm never going to leave you. Not ever." Jocko walked over to Annie and rested his hands on her shoulders. "We got too much going right here. I don't have a desire to see New Jersey again…family? None of them live on the home place anyways." Jocko returned to his chair and sat.

"I'll write her a letter now, iffen you can wait a minute, Henry. Annie can give you another piece of pie and put some heavy cream on it."

Henry nodded his agreement, and Jocko went for a piece of white notepaper and an envelope. He would pay Henry for the postage to be applied in Philipsburg when Henry returned from the mail route.

"I don't mean to be a bad hostess, Henry, but do you mind if I check my mail, too?" ask Annie.

"Of course not, Annie. You go right ahead. It looks like you got some kind of an invitation to something." Henry wore pinch nose, gold wire-rimmed glasses. He carried them in a vest pocket in a hard case. He had put them on his face while looking through Annie's mail. "Do you need help reading your mail, Annie?"

Annie bristled.

"I've been readin' and writin' since I was a youngun, Henry. I don't need no help from nobody."

She, too, took the white envelopes and fanned them in a semi-circle. She reached for the largest. It was square and had fancy printing, spelling her name correctly. The "A" and "M" letters of her name had special curlicues on the ends of the strokes.

"This one first." Annie carefully slid her finger under the flap, trying not to tear the envelope. She pulled out another envelope that spelled her name again on the front. This time the flap was not glued shut. Annie could hardly keep her hands steady.

"This is an invitation to something fancy, Jocko."

Jocko, busily writing his reply, only murmured "ah-huh" back.

"Oh, my goodness sakes. Laws a-mighty. This invitation is from Mrs. Clarissa Jane Crump, over in Helena." Annie waved the paper in the air.

"Jocko, I've been invited to attend a "Pleasant Hour Club" social to be held in her garden." Annie stopped talking but continued to read. Her eyes moved back and forth, flying over the page, trying to take it all in.

"I met her years back, Jocko, when I spent a few days with the colored folks in Helena on my way over here."

Jocko put down his pencil and looked across the table at Annie. He saw the sparkle in her eyes and heard the excitement, like a child's, in her voice.

"When is it, Annie?"

"In a couple of weeks, when her garden is the fullest. She raises flowers, Jocko. Can you imagine a garden full of roses? I can smell their perfume right now."

Henry coughed. "Yes, we all can smell that perfume. The envelope has been sprayed with rose water. I bet my postbag will be permeated with that scent for some time to come." The three friends laughed, filling the kitchen with a friendly and comfortable sound.

"I won't say I wouldn't want to go and visit with other ladies of color.

"Mrs. Crump is a very important woman in Helena, Jocko. She keeps in touch with us ladies by planning parties, and she is a leader in the St. James Free Methodist-Episcopal Church." Annie didn't want to put the letter down.

"When they meet, they work on a quilt or a project for someone in need. I know they talk about their families and their jobs, too. To think she remembered me after all this time." Annie sighed.

"Open the next one, Annie. We are curious as to what's in it, too."

Annie reached for another white envelope. She opened it and, to her surprise, a one-page, folded letter easily pulled out. She carefully spread it out on the tabletop to read it out loud.

"Why, it is a letter telling us all about Montana Territory becoming the forty-first star on the American flag. We will be citizens of the State of Montana starting November 8, 1889. President Henry Harrison issued the proclamation. There will be celebrations in Helena as well as Virginia City." Annie paused to think about what she had just read.

"*You* will be able to *vote,* Joseph Case." Her voice was so quiet he almost didn't hear her profound words.

"I'll bet there will be some fireworks shot off around the mines over here, too," chimed in Henry. "The politicians will be in good form with speeches about how important their work has been and will be for the "future of our children." Henry raised his right arm and saluted the room. Again, the three laughed a familiar and comfortable laugh.

"Laws, Jocko. We been here all these years? We've survived the Civil War, the Indian Wars, the rugged years on the plains...." She reached across the tabletop to take Jocko's hands into hers.

Henry felt he was intruding upon their 'moment' and squirmed a bit. He looked out the window and noticed the clouds were darkening and looking to pour rain very soon.

"Jocko...we're getting *old!*"

"Aw, Annie. We're timeless. That letter just proves it." He smiled, but then grew serious.

"Would you like to take a trip to Helena in the fall, Annie?" She started to protest, but Jocko held up his right hand, palm out towards her. "Now, just think on it a minute. We've got a stack of checks here, so money to get you there is no problem. I'll stay here and tend to things. You can go to Philipsburg for one night, then to Drummond for another night, and then catch the train over to Helena. You could stay with one of the ladies iffen you couldn't get a room at the Helena Hotel." Jocko looked at Annie. She smiled a loving smile at her dear friend.

"Jocko, you old fool. Do you think I'd take over a week in the fall to go a galavantin' to Helena? Sure, it would be fun to see the ladies again, but my dear man, I am content just to see your ugly mug every mornin'. She thought a minute. Then she laughed.

Jocko folded his letter into the envelope and wrote his niece's address on the front of it. He had quickly penned his niece that he would not be visiting in the east, at least not this fall.

He looked for Henry, who sat, patiently waiting for Jocko's letter.

"Forgive us, Henry. We shouldn't be discussin' this in front of you. But, news is so excitin' and as you know, we don't get much mail way out here. Thank you for puttin' up with our silliness." Annie stood up when Henry did.

"Oh, don't give it another thought. But, if you're finished, Jocko, I best be on my way. I'm staying the night with the Meyers' in their bunkhouse. It's still a five-mile ride to their place. My missus doesn't like me riding around in the dark this time of the year. She made arrangements with Mrs.

Meyers some time back, and I appreciate not having that long ride back into town. You folks are a long ways back into this mountain, you know?" Henry raised his right arm towards the window. "Looks like rain will be falling here soon, too."

Jocko and Annie stood in the yard and waved goodbye to Henry.

Without another word, Jocko returned to the fields to tend to the horses he had left tied to the mower. He'd try to finish the last round before the rain, or darkness overtook him. Annie went back into the cabin. She picked up the checks and put them into the coffee tin that she kept on the shelf. The letter from Jocko's niece she leaned against Jocko's brush on the dresser top.

With just one more glance at the fancy writing on the invitation, Annie tossed the letter inside her dresser drawer. *One good thing, the rosewater scent will freshen up this here drawer for a while,* she thought.

# ~ 24 ~

▼

# ANNIE

## 1913 - 1914

Like pages on a beautiful, mountain-scene calendar, Jocko and Annie worked their lives in the rhythmic pattern only nature, and the passing of time, could provide.

Neither were aware how swiftly that passage of time had come upon them, and they entered their twilight years energetically.

Annie's most valuable and prized possession remained the very first gift Jocko had ever given her. She loved her treadle sewing machine. Over the years, she likened the blending of needle and thread to the chain stitch of their lives. One stitch to another stitch until the chain represented their accomplishments and, most importantly, the commitment made to each other through their common-law marriage. Neither ever even considered breaking their "let's shake-on-it." It was as if a beautiful tapestry spread before her when occasionally she would recall the events that occurred over thirty-five years of memories they had built together.

Both were blessed with good health, and thankfully few accidents occurred. Annie could handle most occurrences with herbs, using her doctoring skills.

Jocko, always the mountain man, usually went on horseback into the high mountain country in search of game and hides when Jack Frost left crystal messages in the windowpane. He was enticed away when fall spread her bronze, orange and rust leaves. The crisp smell of autumn matched the chill in the air, and Jocko would become restless.

When nature called him into the mountains, Annie accepted his need to escape into the wilderness. However, over the years, even these trips became few and far between. Then the unthinkable arrived. A painful arthritis attack hit Jocko, and he did not mention a hunting trip to her that fall. No mention of hunting was discussed ever again, and Annie knew the hunting days were through for Jocko.

Specific activities prepared them for the seasons; especially the cold blasts of winter storms that raged outside their cabin. Inside, however, winter offered the necessary respite for Annie to read the stack of books borrowed from Judge Durfee every fall and returned every spring. She used these long winter afternoons to complete her knitting projects.

In the fall of 1913, Jocko and Annie made their annual trip to Philipsburg. Annie, now eighty years of age, had penciled out her will to take to the county attorney for typing and signatures. She also left a handwritten copy of her will in her coffee can on the shelf in the old barn for safekeeping. Unfortunately, she failed to sign either of the penciled copies.

One provision was that she left her newly acquired black horse to the attorney as payment for her funeral. She requested to be buried on the homestead. (The request to be buried on the homestead was not honored.)

"See you in the spring," said Annie, as she left the courthouse with Jocko. She linked her arm in his and said, "Let's go get us a beer."

## Spring - 1914

During the wee hours of April 8, 1914, a typical Montana spring day, Annie Morgan departed this earth.

Annie never had the opportunity to sign the will declaring that she was leaving everything to Joseph Case. Montana law would not allow him to take possession.

The hardest trip of his whole life had been when he put Annie's lifeless body into her wagon and hitched up the team to take them into Philipsburg. Apparently her heart of gold just gave out during the night. Its constant beating for eighty-one plus years suddenly stopped.

Jocko had turned off on the lane at the Meyers Ranch five miles down the road to tell them about Annie.

"Don't worry about nothin' at the ranch, Jocko. I'll go over and feed the stock, tend to things that need to be done. You stay as long as you need to in Philipsburg." Jack Meyers gave Jocko's hand a hard squeeze.

Jocko was grateful for the neighbor's offer to take care of things. He had not thought about anything but taking care of his Annie.

"I'll be back when it's over," said Jocko as he clicked the team into moving on down the lane.

The first place he stopped when he got to Philipsburg was the doctor's home and office. A lantern burned in Doc Merrill's parlor, and that glow of light gave some comfort to Jocko. The urgent knocking brought the doctor swiftly to Jocko's aid.

"Jocko, I believe Annie probably had a heart attack. I'm putting that on her death certificate."

He wrote swiftly on an official form and signed his name. "Can you give me some information about Annie? When was she born, does she have any relatives? Things like that?"

Jocko sat, stonily cold himself. He answered as best he could, remembering that Annie Morgan had been born in the Maryland area.

"I think she said she was born on a plantation in 1833, maybe 1834. She and her mother worked on a plantation. She became a freed slave. She had cooked and worked for General George Armstrong Custer during the Civil War. As far as I know, Annie never married." Jocko drew a deep breath and sighed. "Except for our common law marriage that lasted for thirty-five years."

"She never had any children. She came into Montana Territory in 1876. She had been one of four domestics to Mrs. Libby Custer when they lived in the Dakota Territory. After General Custer was killed, she left the Little Big Horn with Sandbar Brown and went to Ft. Benton. You knew him. He lived near here."

Jocko looked up from the floor. "Doc, this is stretching me. But I'll continue the best I can."

"You are doing just fine, Jocko." Said the doctor. "Can you tell me more?"

Jocko rubbed his temples.  He waited a moment before answering.

"There were several men riding together and they arrived in Ft. Benton, Montana Territory. Annie rode along with them."

"It was there, in Ft. Benton, that she met Judge Durfee. The judge, who lived part-time in Virginia City, was tending to store business at the time in Ft. Benton. He hired her to move to Philipsburg to take care of his sick uncle. He set them up in the cabin on Rock Creek, some twenty-five miles from Philipsburg. She tended him until he died. The judge paid her with the old cabin. Annie homesteaded the place."

The doctor sat, not interrupting, as Jocko gave the litany of Annie.

The doctor's wife had brought in a coffeepot full of black coffee and a plate of cookies. She discreetly left them on the table by Jocko. He didn't touch the cookies, but he desperately needed the coffee to ward off the chill inside his body.

"What else can I tell you about Annie?" Jocko thought a minute.

"Well, Doc, she saved my hide some thirty-five years ago. I was burning up with the typhoid and wound up on her property up there on Rock Creek. She took me in, and we just lived and loved each other all these years. Doc, we promised not to leave the valley without the other, so I know my girl's still around. She'll wait for me."

The doctor gently led Jocko to the spare bedroom that served as his examining room. Jocko sat, head in hands, tears trickling down his cheeks. He could not believe his Annie had gone without him.

"You need a rest, dear man. I'll take care of Annie from here on." He left a lantern on the table. "The outhouse is out the kitchen door."

The doctor gently closed the door to Jocko's room and sighed. It had been a long day, and now it was going to be a long night. He'd need to put up the team of horses at the livery stable and see to that payment.

He walked out to the wagon, only to find a dog curled up beside Annie. *That might give me some trouble. I better get some leather gloves and a piece of rope to keep the dog from running away or maybe biting me.*

He left the house after a quick word with his wife, saying that he had things to tend to for Annie Morgan. His first stop would be the undertaker's funeral parlor.

# ~ 25 ~

▼

# Joseph "Jocko" "Fisher Jack" Case

## 1915 - 1930

Jocko sat on an old wooden chair that he found in the barn. He stretched his legs full out onto a bale of hay and smoked his pipe. He watched the curlicues of smoke rise up past his Donegal tweed cap towards the rafters of the barn.

*I've done okay on this here homestead. I never ever imagined myself being a property owner. Thanks to my girl, that is. Even after all this time, I can't believe she's gone.* Jocko rubbed his leg, hoping to relieve some of the pain he now had in his knees.

*"A touch of the rheumatiz,"* Annie would've said, as she'd rub horse liniment on his aching back and shoulders. *Her medicines always kept me going. Guess I better go get the liniment and dose my knees.* Jocko laughed. *She put that smelly stuff all over me, but it worked.*

Jocko, not wanting to move just yet, continued to smoke his pipe and reminisce there in the barn he had helped build over thirty-five years ago. *Annie said she wanted a barn to last for 100 winters and, by golly, I think we built one that will go past that.*

For several years after Annie's passing, Jocko had worked to dig out a garage on the other side of the road. He had developed a real interest in a new-fangled machine called an automobile. One of the most exciting days of his life was the day he ordered the Austin automobile.

His very first car, a 1915 conventional 5-litre 4-cylinder model Austin with chain drive, was painted a bright lemon yellow and had a convertible black top. It seemed to Jocko that he was flying down the country lane. When Jocko passed by a neighboring farm, he'd toot the ooga horn and wave to farmers out in their fields. Jocko felt good to be free with the wind blowing in his face. He wore his Donegal tweed cap, the very first gift from Annie, fulfilling her prediction that he would wear the cap all his life. His new companion was a black terrier dog with stand-up, scruffy ears. Jocko named him Bucko. The dog wandered in one day that spring of 1914 and never left.

With the acquisition of the automobile, Jocko was able to make frequent trips into Philipsburg. He had friends to share stories with at the White Front Saloon, and he always checked the board hanging on the wall to see whose fishing trip had ended up with their vehicle sinking through the ice on Georgetown Lake. (This activity became a contest of sorts until the authorities put a stop to it.)

Jocko also kept many meetings with the county attorney in charge of filing homestead papers on the Morgan homestead. Annie had left it all to Jocko in her will, but because the will had not been signed, Jocko had to file his own papers and work the land for five years. Jocko had met every requirement, and now the homestead was officially his.

One concern during the summer season was wildfires. Whenever Jocko was out joy riding, he made note of the fire line scars caused by the 1910 fire that nearly wiped out every rancher in the valley.

Because of that 1910 fire, the federal government started the National Forest Service to protect the forests from future devastation. The men, called rangers, took their jobs seriously. "Fire spotted by 10 a.m., out by 10 p.m." was their official motto. Men spent their summer months living in fire towers located on the highest peaks. Their job was to spot smoke and relay the activity to ground forces, who would then physically put out the fire.

Just the same, in the dry summers, Jocko kept a sharp eye out for forgotten campfires along Rock Creek. He always carried a shovel and bucket in the back of the Austin. Many times over the years, Jocko had saved the valley from potentially dangerous fires.

The years passed by for Jocko, and he reluctantly knew he needed to make some changes in his lifestyle. When the aches and joint pain got to be too much, Jocko started to winter in Philipsburg at a local boarding house. As he aged, he realized the time had come to sell the beloved homestead. With a heavy heart, he struck a deal with the J.W. Meyers Ranch and sold the place for $3,200.

Jocko, always independent, made arrangements to enter the Old Soldier's Home at Columbia Falls, Montana. Just a few short months before his death on March 27, 1930, he left a penciled note.

*Don't send me back east for burial, but take me to the Philipsburg Cemetery and put me near my Annie.*

His wish was granted. He was the last surviving G.A.R. veteran from Granite County. He had participated in every Memorial Day Parade until 1929. Joseph "Jocko" "Fisher Jack" Case was laid to rest near his beloved friend Agnes Annie Morgan.

# THE CABIN
# IN
# THE WOODS

## 2007 – 2009

# Table of Contents

This Book is dedicated to the firefighters
on the Sawmill Complex Fires of 2007

Patrick E. McKelvey
Public Information Officer
Northern Rockies Incident Management Team

# ～ I ～

▼

# FIREFIGHTERS
# 2007

## *Saw Mill Complex-Rock Creek Fire, near Philipsburg, Montana*

The mobile two-way radiophone jangled in the older man's backpack.

"Why does it always sound so darn urgent?" he mumbled to his partner as he reached to retrieve the phone.

"Yeah! Yeah! What's the emergency this time?"

"Where are you two clowns, anyway?" asked the voice, booming so loudly that both men could hear clearly.

"We're walkin' the road near Rock Creek, gettin' very near to the Morgan-Case cabin."

"Right on. You two get over there pronto. The crew is wrapping that cabin and they need help." The voice cut off, and the two men stared at each other.

"Just our luck. Let's keep walking. That cabin has to be near here." The older man started walking backwards, as if trying to spot a landmark or something familiar to him.

"My great-grampa James used to come over here by horseback to camp out and go fishing. He and an old coot named "Fisher Jack" were buddies. They swapped war stories and lied about who caught the biggest fish that got away."

"War stories? What war was your great-grandpa in? The American Revolution?" The men laughed easily at the joke.

"It is a bit confusing, isn't it? I had a Great-grampa James, a Grampa James, and my dad's name is James. My mother said there were enough James's in the family for God to have to sort out on judgment day, and she insisted I have another Irish name." Sean chuckled. "My middle name is James."

"When the twins were born, I teased my wife by telling her we were going to name them James and Jimmy. She didn't think that was one bit funny." He chuckled again as he remembered the conversation about naming the twins twelve years ago.

"Actually, to keep it straight when we talked about our family lineup, we called

Great-grampa James 'Gramps.' I think Gramps James and Fisher Jack Case were both in the Civil War…yeah." The men kept walking at an even pace.

"Gramps James was only sixteen when he fought in that war." The men were getting warmer as they continued to walk up the dirt road.

"My dad wasn't even born yet when all this fishing was going on. But whenever he'd go to visit the old man in the old folks' home, Gramps would spend a lot of time telling him about this guy who lived on Rock Creek and what a great fisherman he was. It would have been neat to have met him."

The men each reached for their water bottles and took a swig before continuing on their path.

"We've been at this fire fighting all day, and I was hoping to find a crew with a truck so we could hitch a ride back to camp. I'd trade one of the twins for a shower and a hot meal."

"Yeah? Well, hold that thought 'cause there's the cabin."

The men stared at the "cabin" in question.

"What the heck? It's ready to fall down on its own self, and we've gotta save it? The fire isn't even on this side of the river. That's nuts." But the two men hurried across the road, and waved to the crew captain.

Joining the crew, they each grabbed a heavy roll of the thick aluminum foil and slid rolls of duct tape up their arms.

"Glad to see you finally made it to the party. Start on the north side," said the crew captain. "Pretend it's a valentine gift for your significant other."

"Ha. Ha. Very funny," said the crew in unison. "We've heard that one before." But they laughed at the idea of wrapping this particular rat-invested cabin to present as a gift to someone special in their lives. One firefighter, however, made a mental note and filed it away in the backside of his brain. *This will look mighty fine next July. Maybe my boys and I can come fishin', like Gramps used to do.*

The crew worked in sync, two to a team, putting the shiny side of the awkward rolls of aluminum foil against the exterior boards. They taped the seams with duct tape.

"How many rolls of this stuff have we used just this week?" asked one of the men.

"You must be new to this fire. We don't even stop to count rolls any more. I stopped counting about 50 houses back." He waved his arms in the air in circles. "This one is a snap of a

job. Earlier today we had to wrap a two-story starter castle…
just keep pulling the tape so we can finish up here."

"Uh, hey, uh…do any of you guys feel like we're being
watched?"

The crew captain stopped in his tracks, and looked at the
young crewmember.

"Heck, yeah. Ole' Smokey Bear is sitting on that ridge
right up there, with a pair of binoculars." He pointed his
index finger at the kid and acted like he was pulling the
trigger on a gun.

"What are you thinking about…ghosts in the bushes?
There ain't nobody around but us. Now get back to work."

The men were feeling the heat of the day and the ash from
the fire. The river would hold back the ground flames but, if
some of that flying ash jumped the water and landed in the
grass then the men were sitting ducks caught this far back up
the canyon.

They were well-trained firefighters. They knew how to
read any given situation where wind, flame, heat of the day
and time of day all came together to form a combustible
possibility. Right now, it was crucial they get their job done
and pack up within the hour.

Usually, the fire evened out and slowly burned during
the darkest hours of the night. The wind would calm down,
which helped the firefighters to get some rest.

There remained a certain beauty in watching the black
skyline burn orange and red, as flames crested the top of
a nearby mountain. Even the most grizzled and seasoned
firefighter occasionally became mesmerized by the action of
the always reaching, constantly moving flames.

Daylight, however, brought back reality. Thousands of acres became useless landscape after the dragonfire roared through.

More than once the main camp had to be evacuated when the wind shifted, sending a surprise fire their direction. The men did not want any of that action tonight.

"Time's up!" shouted the crew captain. "Let's wrap up and get out of here." He waved his bright-yellow-jacketed arm over his head in an arc, and pointed toward the truck.

They surveyed their job. The fire had stayed on the other side of Rock Creek, but the mountain had long blotted out the sunlight. Trapped smoke and an eerie darkness quickly surrounded them. The men were exhausted from the exertion of wrapping the cabin. Their lungs burned from breathing the heavy, putrid smoke. None of the crew wore facemasks, claiming they just got in their way.

The men climbed into the van, filling in the back seats first, making room for the two extra firefighters.

"You know what I'm going to do next summer?" The older firefighter rubbed his black-rimmed, raccoon eyes with a calloused hand as he climbed into the van, sitting next to his buddy. "I'm going to bring my twin sons back here to do some serious fishin'."

"If we ever get this fire under control, you mean." His buddy jabbed him in the ribs. "Hey! Give us another week and pray for rain. I'm ready to get out of this here army."

Most of the men were comfortable with each other after spending nearly five months in the same firefighting crew during Montana's wildfire season. This year's season began late in May due to several years of drought. No rain had fallen all spring and summer.

The firefighters were weary. This fire was taking its toll, both physically and mentally, but an end was in sight. The predicted fall rains would be the angels of the fire fighters.

The ride back to the main camp was long, as the dirt road was in need of gravel and full of potholes. The driver tried singing "ninety-nine bottles of beer on the wall, ninety-nine bottles of beer," but gave it up after a couple of cat calls and boos from the men in the back. All they wanted was a quick ride back to camp, a hot shower, a good cup of strong coffee, and a four-course meal.

"Yeah! Pray for that rain."

Morgan-Case Homestead Cabin foil wrapped and saved by Firefighting crew – 2007

## ~ 2 ~

▼

# JULY 2008

The road leading in to the Hog Back-Rock Creek area had not been graded nor had the potholes been filled in. A hard winter dropped an extraordinary snowfall during December, January and February. The natural cycle was complete. The burnt grasses of last fall had recovered nicely, and restoration was evident.

Sean noticed that the farmers had already put up a first hay crop. Large bales, still spread across the meadows, waited to be stacked up. Most of the signs of the unquenchable wildfire, belching like a bloodthirsty dragon consuming and devouring everything in its path, had disappeared.

Mother Earth had painted a pretty face with new grasses and wild flowers. Only the stands of charred, blackened tree trunks remained as a reminder to the firefighter returning to the scene of his job the summer before.

Sean enjoyed his years as a firefighter. He began his career with the Forest Service the summer he graduated from high school. He had saved his wages and it had help pay for his college tuition at Carroll College in Helena. After graduation, he married his high school sweetheart, Judy. They agreed that he should continue to sign on as a firefighter during the summer months.

His assignments had included fire spotting from a tower high on a mountaintop. It was a lonely job, but nature supplied him with plenty of activity. Wild animals visited him daily. He learned to take great photos of bears, mountain lions, elk, deer and whatever wandered into his tower area. He spent the day and evening hours searching the skyline for that telltale puff of smoke.

For the past fifteen years, during the school season, Sean had taught mathematics at Helena High School. But come spring, he always signed up for another fire season. Judy was a good sport about his being gone so much on fire calls during the summer. The money he made went into the college fund for their twin boys.

This year was different. He wanted to spend time with his twins. Kinden and Kevin, twelve years old on their last birthday in March, needed a summertime dad.

For Christmas gifts, Sean decided he'd plan a fishing trip for himself and the twins only. He purchased fishing equipment and outfitted the two boys with the best brands Capitol Sports Store carried. He called and reserved the Morgan-Case cabin for a week in July, through the U.S. Forest Service office in Missoula, Montana. This would be a special time with his boys.

Sean drove carefully around the potholes, weary of the swirling yellow dust that filled every inch inside the new Subaru Outback. He was very much aware of his unwilling passengers. He tried to loosen them up a bit.

"Look how high the flames rose on those trunks over there."

He pointed to a stand of pines weaving in the wind, leaning into each other.

Kevin stared straight ahead. The ride proved long, dusty and teeth jarring to him. He didn't want to be here. He wanted to be back home with his little league baseball team. Never mind that for the past couple of months he'd sat out all the games on the bench. He wanted to hang out with his friends.

Kinden sat up and looked out the windows. He looked at the burnt tree trunks his dad had just pointed out to them.

"Yep. It sure is pretty back in here," said Kinden. "Can we fish right away? How much longer, Dad?"

Sean doubted he would ever understand how these two boys could be identical twins, yet have such different personalities. Kinden had always shown an interest in the outdoors, hunting, fishing, camping, working in the yard, and enjoying sports at school. Kinden's shelves held sports trophies, team photos, and ribbons won in baseball and soccer.

Kevin, however, enjoyed computers, art and drama, and he had already been named the school's best reader in the reader's group. He liked to mentor younger kids who had reading problems. Books filled his room's shelves. Already, he wore glasses.

Sean glanced over at his frustrated young son. "You should have seen it last year when I was here fightin' the big fire. Flames shot up over a hundred feet high and smoke was touchin' the bottom sides of airplanes flyin' over for a look-see."

Kevin shifted enough to stare out the side window and, even though he spotted a couple of deer near his side of the road, he didn't comment.

"Cool!" said Kinden from his back seat.

"We were one happy bunch of firefighters when we started the mop up. That welcome-rainstorm comin' over the mountain was a sight to see. We were worried it might set off more fires, the way the sky was lighting up from the electric strikes. Heck, that fire might still be smolderin' in some of the downed tree roots. We can hike to some and take some scientific notes."

The all-wheel-drive Subaru bumped along for another mile until Sean stopped at a bridge.

"Here is the marker I was lookin' for."

He turned the rig to the left, continuing to follow the river on the driver's side of the road.

"This is a blue-ribbon fishin' stream, boys. We'll be eatin' fish for breakfast tomorrow. Want to bet me who pulls out the biggest fish first?"

"I'll bet I win," shouted Kinden, excited at the prospect of being on the river very soon.

Kevin continued to ignore his dad. He was not even thankful for the cold drink Sean had thoughtfully brought out to the boys when they stopped for gasoline and sacks of ice at a station near the outskirts of Philipsburg. When they left the highway for the dirt road, the extremely fine, yellow dust swirled inside the vehicle even though the windows were up. The air conditioning was set on high. The drink settled some of the dust in Kevin's parched throat, but he felt trapped in his seat belt. He squirmed around to scratch his itchy back.

"How much longer until we find this spot of yours, Dad?"

They had left Helena only a few hours earlier, but to Kevin it seemed a lifetime ago. This whole fishing vacation idea had not been Kevin's doing. The boy liked occasionally being outdoors, camping with the family, but the timing for this campout just wasn't right. For one thing, he and his dad were not the best of friends like they used to be. Kevin wanted to hang out with his buddies, not be isolated somewhere on a river trying to catch fish with his old man.

One rule for campouts had always been "no cell phones, no computers, and no battery-operated games." But board games, cards, puzzles and books were allowed. His cell phone wouldn't work at the base of this mountain. To go all week without his computer was asking too much. He had hoped for a new wireless laptop for Christmas, not fishing gear.

"Not much longer…There! There is the cabin…and the gate's waitin' for you to get out and swing it open." Sean turned left, barely missing a large USFS historical marker sign introducing the campers to the Morgan-Case rental cabin.

Kevin unhooked his seatbelt glad to finally be free. He jumped out of his seat when the Subaru came to a halt. He stood on tiptoe and pushed up on the wire loop. It proved to be extra tight, but Sean remained behind the wheel, letting his son wrestle with it. One last chest hug to the pole, and the wire loop popped upward.

"Look! Dad, I got it!" Then Kevin impulsively surprised his dad. He hooked his left foot onto the bottom pole of the gate and, with a push from his other foot, he rode the gate as it swung across the grass in the roadway leading to the cabin.

Sean hid his smile. *Maybe the kids will like bein' out here with dumb dad after all? One can only hope,* he thought as he drove on through the open gate.

"Dad! This is great. Wow! What a spot. You told me you were driving to a dump of a cabin. Wow! Are we at the right place?" asked Kinden, still strapped in his back seat.

Sean did a double take. Yes, this was the right cabin. However, it was restored: completely repainted, glassed-in windowpanes. A porch and a ramp led up to the new door.

The hands of volunteers had renovated the cabin, earlier in the year. It was now on the National Registry as a homestead from another century. The Forest Service sponsors a website that lists restoration projects in the national forests that brings both men and women as volunteers from all over the country. They spend two weeks working on restoration as instructed by the foreman of the job.

The work had been completed in record time. The Forest Service controlled the destiny of the cabin now, and rental days are available for a fee. It was through this rental program that Sean had secured this week in July.

He recognized the bunkhouse, the water pump in the yard, and the dugout across the way. The remnants of the old saw mill were still littered out in the field. Ancient lilac bushes stood guard at the front, screened-in porch. Virginia creeper vines entwined up the corner posts of the porch and crawled across the roofline. The unforgettable scent of honeysuckle greeted the renters as they passed by on the stone walkway.

Sean looked to his left, towards the bunkhouse. He wondered if it was rented out, too. He started to walk over to the bunkhouse to check it out, but his sons called him back.

"Come on, Dad. Let's see inside."

Kinden ran up the path and tried the door. It was locked.

"Here! Catch!" shouted Sean.

Kinden caught the key and inserted it easily into the lock. He pushed the door open and stepped inside, letting the screen door slam behind him. Kevin ran in behind him.

"Hurry up, Dad. This is a great place!" Kinden raced through the small rooms. "I get first dibs on where I sleep."

Sean, loaded down with gear, looked for the wooden kitchen table to set down the tackle box. He stood inside the cabin alongside Kinden.

"Yep. We firefighters wrapped the right place. Just for us, boys. Come on, let's get the stuff inside before a bear smells our bacon."

Kinden jerked around and smiled at his Dad. He started to give him a hug, but changed his mind and went outside for another load of gear.

## ~ 3 ~
▼

# COMPANY ARRIVES

The river gurgled as it swirled around the huge boulders that gave it the name Rock Creek. Annie sat on the stump of a windfall pine tree, toppled since 1880. She thought she heard a motorcar's engine, an unfamiliar sound to her untrained ears. However, the rushing swift waters muffled the sounds, and Joseph didn't even look up when she called out to him.

Annie Morgan and Joseph Case had enjoyed living at this location during their lifetime. They had promised each other, over one hundred years ago, that they would spend time in their spirit world together, vacationing at their homestead on Rock Creek. Annie often said that even "God vacationed here, because it was just the perfect spot in all of Montana."

"Jocko, I hear a motorcar approachin'. Come in, and let's go check the cabin yard." Annie stood up and brushed her calico dress before she took a step toward the meadow's edge.

"Joseph, did you hear me?"

The one thing Joseph Case loved to do was fish. Sometimes, he became so absorbed in his private thoughts, mesmerized by the swirling waters, that he shut out Annie's voice all together. Annie called him Jocko, he figured, as kind of a lover's name. But when he heard "Joseph," he'd snap back to reality.

- - - - - - -

Joseph had another name, "Fisher Jack." The miners and railroad men all called him by that name. In his earlier days, he had supplied their camps with wild game that the cooks could toss into the cooking pot. In turn, he was paid a handsome wage. He'd jokingly told the agents he didn't make enough to buy his bullets.

He'd skin the animals, dry the pelts, and make another sale off the hides. Bear, deer, moose, elk, the big cats, even gophers and squirrels, all found their demise if Jocko would sight them wandering through the meadows, or in the valley, where Flint Creek meandered through the willows. He had hunted every day year round, always bringing trophy game slung over the rump of the packhorse.

After joining up with Annie on the homestead, Jocko had made the decision to hunt only occasionally, as there was plenty of work that needed his attention on the homestead. He was contented to have the confined life with Annie, knowing he'd have a warm bed, a good meal, and companionship waiting at the end of the workday.

His fishing passion began as a kid back in New Jersey in the 1850's. His family lived out on a farm that had a small pond. He had watched wild ducks and geese fly over, landing in their fields during the birds' migration every fall.

The pattern repeated itself in the spring. It was an idyllic time in Joseph's young life. He hunted with his older brother, Terrence. The boys, along with their dad, fished, and hunted deer, squirrels, and other wild game, to provide meat for the family table. He took great pride in his shooting skills. Little did he know it would provide him with his life's work.

Suddenly, the year was 1860. Rumors of war between the North and the South echoed inside the walls of the local general mercantile store. The war interrupted his young life of sixteen years.

The lure of joining up with the Irish Brigade filled his imagination with thoughts of glory. Thomas Francis Meagher, Jr., the Irish "Orator" from New York City, had journeyed to New Jersey where he cajoled and promised at the same time. The call of the "wild geese" was stronger than the young man could resist. Joseph joined the Union cause. He was assigned to General Thomas Francis Meagher's Irish Brigade when he first joined up, but as the war continued, he found himself a part of General George A. Custer's group. In the latter years, he was transferred into General William Tecumseh Sherman's unit. This unit marched through the South to Georgia and the sea. The plan, known as the Savannah Campaign, conducted in late 1864, wrought destruction as they burned everything in their path, and this campaign helped to bring an end to the war.

Joseph Case became a lost soul at the end of the war. He drifted west, looking for General Meagher. He would sign up for Injun fighting.

- - - - - - -

"Joseph! Come on." Annie waved her arm high over her head to catch his attention. "What are you thinking about? We have company…. again."

Joseph wound the line back into his reel and waded across the knee-high water, careful not to slip. He knew every inch of this river, even from the rocky side up. He hurried to catch up with Annie, also curious to see the newcomers.

"They drive a nice outfit. You remember how I liked the fancy cars, Annie? I wish you could have been alive to ride with me. I had some good times riding over to Philipsburg during the summer months in that old Austin."

"Oh, you old fool. That was a long time ago," said Annie. She smiled, remembering the yellow and black convertible that Jocko loved to drive. He had hand-built the dugout across the road from the cabin to serve as a garage for his dream car.

As the two ambled toward the yard, Jocko caught site of Sean, struggling to unload the outfit in one trip.

"That man…he looks familiar to me." Jocko shook his head and looked again. "I must be getting senile or something. How could I know this guy…  Annie?"

Just then two boys, identical twins, burst out of the cabin with the screen door banging behind them.

"Let's go check out the river," yelled one to the other.

Oblivious to their surroundings, the two young boys, about twelve years of age or so, ran right past the invisible couple.

"Well, this might be interesting. Shall we let them see us?" asked Annie.

"I'm game if you are. There is something about this group. I just can't put my finger on it. Those boys are going to be a handful. Let's go see how long they plan to stay in our cabin, and play in our meadows."

"Don't forget the apple trees and strawberries." Annie was smiling at the idea of having the younguns to entertain. There were all kinds of ways for the two of them to get into some mischief. She felt it would be good for Jocko, too.  He could teach them about fishing.

Tossing small rocks into the river occupied the twins. They walked along the bank, surprised at the rush of the water.

"When we get back to the cabin, let's unwrap all our fishin' gear so it's ready in the morning." Said Kevin. "It's too late to go fishing tonight, and the mosquitoes are biting me something fierce." He slapped at his bare arms and neck. Sunup will come mighty early out here with Dad, remember."

Kevin tossed another smooth stone into the river. The kerplunk sound interrupted the flowing gurgles and neither boy heard or saw the older couple. They were almost upon them at the bend of the river.

"Hello, boys. How's fishin'?" asked Jocko, as he extended his hand for them to shake. Annie stood back a step or two, and smiled a broad, welcoming smile.

The boys were surprised to meet people this late in the summer evening, but the river was open to all fishermen. These two were probably just passing through on their way to their own campsite.

Kinden, the more adventurous of the twins, started visiting right away. Kevin held back, observing the couple standing before him. *Look at the way that guy is dressed. Those laced up boots come to his knees...and that hat...it's all covered with hand tied flies.* Kevin looked at the bamboo rod, and the reel wound with heavy line. *Wow! This guy looks like he stepped out of a museum or something. And look at her head, wrapped up like the lady on the syrup bottle.*

Kevin pulled on Kinden's sleeve. "Come on, Kinden. Dad's going to miss us. It's starting to get dark, and we have to help him unload the SUV."

"Oh, yeah. Nice talking to you. Maybe we will see you in the morning?"

"Yes, for sure. We'll be fishin' for our breakfast by dawn's light," said Annie. We love fresh fish right out of this cold river water. Uuumm, uumm."

The twins turned back the way they had come, surprised at how far away they were from the cabin. When Kevin started to run, Kinden hurried to catch up.

"What's the rush, Kevin? Hey! Wait for me."

Annie and Jocko, pleased with their joke on the two boys, walked on past the cabin, not even peeking inside like they normally did. They now lived in the bunkhouse, located a short distance to the left of the Morgan-Case cabin. Like the caretakers they were, they kept track of the people who came to vacation on the Morgan-Case Homestead Property.

"I think these three will take care of our cabin, Annie. We can plan on spending time with those boys and give their Dad some time to fish."

Jocko started to hum an Irish pub tune. The song carried on the night air. The vacationers looked out the window at the same time and noticed a lantern glow coming from the bunkhouse.

"Gee, Dad. We got company," said Kinden. "They look awful old to be out fishing," said Kevin. The twins looked at each other, but just shrugged.

"I'll have a talk with them tomorrow, guys." Sean stepped back from the window and sat at the kitchen table. "Let's get some sleep. Tomorrow we'll find out about our neighbors to the left of us."

Photo 3 Window frame

# ~ 4 ~

▼

# SIGN BY THE GATE

Sean was awake at the crack of dawn. *Those chirping birds make an annoying alarm clock,* he thought. The twins had talked in muffled voices late into the night, keeping him awake. He thought he had heard them talking about ghosts.

*Maybe they had a comic book they were reading by flashlight under the covers? Well, I'll let the boys sleep in a bit longer. The coffee brewing will raise them out of their cots soon enough.*

Sean had just returned from an urgent trip to the outhouse. It was chilly out, and he was glad he had pulled on his jeans, jacket, and boots before venturing out.

The unexpected knock at the door startled him. There, standing on the wood-planked front porch, stood an odd-looking couple: a white man and a black woman, both dressed in old clothes as if from another century.

"Hello…can I help you?" Sean asked as he opened the door. "Come on in and have a cup of coffee."

Sean looked towards the bedroom area. "The boys are still in their bags, but I hear them stirring."

"Oh, no. We were out fishin' early, and saw the smoke comin' from the cook stove. We thought maybe you could use some fresh fish," offered Annie.

Annie had cleaned the fish, and Sean saw they were ready for cornmeal. His mouth started watering at the thought of these fish sizzling in hot bacon grease.

"Why thank you. What a nice surprise." Sean pushed open the screen door. He took the fish string from Annie. He turned back toward the bedroom, and saw the twins standing shyly by the bedroom door.

The couple again declined the invitation, saying they would come another time. They failed to mention that they had met the twins the night before.

Sean held open the screen door, but turned toward the bedroom.

"Boys! Come and meet our neighbors. We've got fresh fish for breakfast."

He turned back to the open door, only to find the couple had vanished from the porch. Curious, Sean walked out onto the planks. He looked left and right, but the couple was nowhere in sight. *Must have gone inside the bunkhouse,* he thought.

The boys, dressed in sweatshirts and pants, had pulled on heavy socks. They were hopping stiff-legged in front of the kitchen stove, trying to warm up. Kinden spotted the mess of fish.

"Dad, did you go fishing already?" He didn't wait for an answer. "I'm hungry…where's the big iron pan?" He rummaged through the cardboard boxes, still packed with gear, and pulled out a huge, iron skillet and a lid.

"Kevin, bring me the bacon from the cooler, so we can cook these up. I need an egg, too." Kinden had already poured out the cornmeal onto a platter. "Thanks, Kevin." He took the egg and cracked it into a bowl. He whipped it with a fork as he talked. Next, he coated the fish, waiting for the bacon to heat up.

"Where did you learn to cook fish, Kinden?" Sean was surprised at how his son took over the kitchen so easily.

"Gee, Dad. We've been camping with Mom…forever," said Kinden. "We know how to do lots of stuff out in the woods. You just haven't been around us much." Kinden flipped over the lightly golden, fried fish to give the other side a chance to fry.

"Mom takes us to Park Lake and stuff, you know." He had removed the bacon strips from the pan and put them on a piece of paper to drain. He planned to save them for BLTs later in the day.

That last zinger struck Sean like a jab to the heart. He knew the boy meant no disrespect. They understood that the money Sean made at the firefighting job was necessary to their household. But he was, now more than ever, glad he had made the decision to skip firefighting this summer. He needed this time with the boys.

Sean watched his sons working together. Soon the delicious, sizzling fish smell filled the cabin, and the three sat at the wooden table. Kevin had poured glasses full of orange juice, and made toasted bread. Jam and butter were on the table, too.

"You boys did the cookin'. I'll do the cleanin' up." Sean reached for a potholder and wrapped it around the handle of the metal coffee pot. He poured himself one more cup. With his coffee cup in one hand, and a kitchen chair in the other, he walked out the door.

"I'm goin' to sit out here and soak in some mornin' rays for a while."

The twins fell over each other, trying to find their boots in the already jumbled up bedroom. Sean had emptied out the Subaru, and had set their boxes of "stuff" on the floor in the bedroom area. It was up to the boys to make some sense of the mess they brought from home.

Kinden whispered to his brother.

"Kevin, I want to go read that sign that we passed before we turned into the yard. I saw it when I opened the gate yesterday afternoon."

"Why? What do you think you are going to read on that sign?"

"I don't know. But there is something mighty peculiar about that couple we met last night, don't you think? Did you see them, really look at them?" Kinden reached for a note pad and a ballpoint pen.

"Let's go."

The boys waved to Sean as they jumped off the other edge of the porch, and disappeared around the side of the cabin. They walked quickly up the stone path to stand in front of the sign.

Kinden quickly read the words and made some notes on his pad.

"I've got the willies, Kevin."

"Oh! Gag. Are you sick? Please say you aren't sick." Kevin reached for his brother's arm. "If you *are* sick, we will have to go home."

"No, you dumb-head. I'm not that kind of sick. I think we have just landed in the twilight zone." Kinden pointed to the words again.

"This is a National Registry location, Kevin. A white man, Joseph Case and a black woman, Agnes Annie Morgan, homesteaded the place. Look at that date."

Kevin did pay attention now. "Kinden, do you suppose…?" He shook his head, his eyes the size of silver dollars. "Naw… Naw…Kinden? What do you think? Do you think? Naw….

Do you think they haunt their home ground and kill boys who come to visit?"

Kinden rolled his eyes, and looked at Kevin.

"Well, if I am right, then that funny-looking couple we met last night is Annie and Joseph. I have read that people haunt places where they were happy in life. They are ghosts. You know, like we see on TV sometimes."

"I'm not afraid…are you afraid, Kinden?

"I'm not afraid…if you're not afraid," he answered his twin.

Kevin punched Kinden's arm and tried to push him into the tall grass.

"Let's not tell Dad what we think we know. He'd make us go home.

Now that we are actually here, I really do want to go fishing." Kevin drew a deep breath. "If we see them again, we ask them who they are. Okay?"

Kinden nodded his head. "I'm *not* afraid, not really. We can ask them to tell us stuff about when they were kids." Then Kinden started to laugh. "We can write a paper when school starts about what we did on our summer vacation."

Sean heard the boys laughing and chasing each other on the other side of the house. *They are havin' a good time already, and the weather is perfect. I'm not going to say anything to them about the odd couple unless it becomes a problem*, he thought.

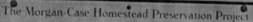

# The Morgan-Case Homestead Preservation Project

The first known occupant of this property was Annie Morgan, who settled here in the late 1800's in a two-room cabin that was part of an abandoned fox farm. Annie was a black woman who came to Montana as a cook for Lt. Col. George Custer in 1876 at the age of 44. In the mid 1800's Annie came across Joseph Case, who was very ill. Morgan nursed Case back to health. She and Case, also known as Fisher Jack, "formed a partnership by which he was to improve the claim and receive an undivided half interest in the claim." Hence the name "Morgan-Case Homestead."

The Missoula Ranger District, Lolo National Forest began preservation work on the Morgan-Case Homestead in April, 2001. You may know this place as Pigear Ranch, which was purchased by Frank and Sarah Poyear in 1951. They cut timber and harvested hay at the ranch until moving away in 1956. The Poyears rented the ranch until 1979, when the U.S. Forest Service purchased the buildings and 320 acres for its recreation values.

This ranch is currently being nominated to the National Register of Historic Places for its significance relating to early homesteading and ranching (1890-1951) in Granite County and Western Montana. It is being preserved to the historic appearance of the 1940's. The homestead is being renovated for use as a Forest Service administrative site and public cabin rental.

This work is being done by the Missoula Ranger District in partnerships with Historical Research Associates (HRA) Historical Architect James McDonald and numerous volunteers working through the Forest Service Passport In Time (PIT) program. For more information, contact the Missoula Ranger District, Lolo National Forest, Bldg 24A, Fort Missoula, Missoula, MT 59804.

# ～ 5 ～

▼

# WATER WHEEL FUN

The sun climbed steadily across the heavens strewn with lazily floating cumulous clouds, casting shadows in the yard and the front side of the cabin. Even the squirrels were resting in the summer heat. Deer were bedded down in the tall meadow grasses. The twins, stripped to their bare chests and swim trunks, were helping their dad make a water wheel out of sticks and tree branches they'd gathered for the project.

"We can't use any nails or glue," said Sean. "But we can use a pocket knife."

"Here's a good length of a lodge pole that we can jump on to snap it into two pieces," said Kevin. "Come on, Kinden. I set it up between these two big rocks. Now, you gotta jump on it."

As Kinden started to climb up on one side of the big boulder, Sean grabbed his arm just in time.

"Don't you do that. You could get hurt. That pole would split all right, but it might come back and clunk you on the back of the head, or poke your eye out."

"Aahh, Dad. Then how are we going to snap this pole in two?" asked Kevin.

"You got me there, son."

Annie and Jocko had been watching the trio as they worked by the river's edge. Kevin felt their presence and glanced up just as Jocko was getting ready to announce himself and Annie.

"Hello!" called Jocko.

"Hey! Mister. You got an ax? We could sure use one," said Kevin.

Jocko walked close up, and produced a very sharp ax.

"Matter of fact, son, I do." He swung the ax off his shoulder and handed it to Sean. "We were just out lookin' for some firewood. You can use it."

With one swing of the ax, Sean cut the section of the lodge pole into two parts. He then used the ax to make a "v" notch in the ends. He shaped the other ends into points, making it easier to poke the poles into the wet bank.

"Thanks. We didn't introduce ourselves this mornin'. My name is Sean Patricks, and my boys are Kevin and Kinden." He handed the ax back to Jocko. "We enjoyed the fish. Thanks again for bringin' them by."

The twins looked at each other and then at their dad. "You brought the fish? We thought Dad caught them before we woke up," said Kevin.

Annie spoke first. "We live along side of you in the bunkhouse. You might have seen our light last night? My name is Annie, and this here is Jocko." They smiled warmly at the twins. "We talked a bit last night with you boys."

The twins nodded a kind of "hello" and returned to their water wheel project. It would be later that they would remember the names from the sign by the gate.

The elderly couple didn't move on. Obviously, they wanted to see what the final outcome of the wood project was going to look like.

"Would you like to stay and watch us make our water wheel?"

Sean asked. He kept an eye on the boys as they were using the pocketknife.

Kevin worked easily with the sharp blade to bore holes around the width of the pole. "This pole will fit into the "v" notches you made, Dad," spoke Kevin.

The boys scratched about in the debris they had accumulated until they found narrow sticks to insert into the bored holes that Kinden had finished.

"We have to push these littler sticks into the holes to make spokes for our water wheel," offered Kinden as he looked up at Jocko. The water wheel now reminded Sean of a bicycle wheel.

Kevin once again picked up the pocketknife. He was pleased with his handiwork so far.

"Now I have to make little slits in the ends of the narrow sticks."

Kinden returned to his search for pieces of thin bark that he could slide easily into the slits. "See, Annie? We now have pretend buckets to catch the water as the wheel goes around in the water."

Annie clapped her hands. "My, my, what clever youngsters you are."

Kinden smiled. "I've read that in the olden days, back East, that farmers made huge water wheels like our little model, and put wooden buckets on the ends of each one of the spokes. The buckets filled with water as the river flowed causing the wheel to turn around. Then the buckets dumped the water into a chute that spilled the water into a huge tub or a pool, so the cows could get a drink. Farmers usually fenced off the stream so the animals couldn't stand around in the water."

Sean smiled as he oversaw the scene. His twins were certainly working together on this project, like a matched pair. As usual, Kevin explained the process, but it was Kinden doing the manual labor. It wasn't long before the boys had the water wheel assembled. Kinden waded into the water and jammed the pole as hard as he could down into the mud of the creek. Kinden did the same thing with his pole, only he was standing on the soft bank edge. He wedged his end deeper so the pole was nearly the same height as Kevin's pole.

"Here, Kevin. Grab the end of the cross-pole and let's give this a try." He stretched the cross-pole out over the water to reach Kevin's hand.

"This water is ice cold. Hurry up!"

Now it was up to Kevin. Working together, the boys lowered the water wheel pole to sit in the notched "v" at the same time and, as luck would have it, the spokes holding the "buckets" were long enough to reach the water. Immediately the wheel started spinning.

"Hurray! We did it." The boys were obviously pleased with themselves that their project actually worked.

Sean snapped his pocketknife shut. "It's time to get serious about fishin'." He started walking back toward the cabin to get his gear.

# ~ 6 ~

▼

# FISHING GEAR

Intrigued now to see some new fishing equipment, Jocko and Annie waited near the stream. Their bamboo, two-piece rods had served them well over the years, and Jocko had no plans to ever replace his fishing gear. He liked the simplicity and solidness of his pole, and his reel hand turned easily. He kept it cleaned, and he used a heavy line made from braided silk strips.

Before he changed to the silk line, he had fished with horsetail strands that were braided into a long line. He liked the feel of the bamboo rod. It was what he called "slow action," and it made the rod feel alive when he cast out into the water. He carried his cat-gut leader in a round tin box lined with felt that had to be kept wet or the cat gut would stiffen and break into crumbled pieces.

His creel was willow bush vine that he had twisted and weaved into a lightweight basket, with a leather strap that was long enough to fit around his neck and across his chest. He lined it with moss or leaves and, when fishing, he kept it wet so that when he caught a fish it would stay moist and cool.

Sometimes he carried a net and an extra piece of heavy vine or twig to string out the fish. He kept them submerged in the water until he was through fishing for the day.

He was curious as to what these younguns would bring out for their fishing gear and grew impatient at the delay.

The boys, inside the cabin, were going through the camping boxes looking for all of their packages.

"We were going to unpack this stuff last night, remember?" said Kevin.

They unwrapped graphite rods, hooked the four sections together easily, and slid the reel into the attached reel seat near the cork handgrip. The reels required the boys to hand-wind the nylon filament.

Both boys wore baseball-type caps to shield their eyes, and they each had a canvas bag to put their catch into. The canvas bag would need to be dipped in the river, and be kept wet so that the fish would remain cool and fresh.

"Better grab some mosquito repellent and sun screen," Kevin shouted to Kinden before he headed back out the door. "Have you got your fly box?"

Sean stopped the boys. "Hey! You need to take a bottle of water with you, and don't forget to drink it," he ordered, as he tossed them bottles of water from the huge Coleman cooler.

Armed now with the best fishing equipment their money could buy, the trio returned to where they had left the elderly couple.

"Hhhmmm…they left already," said Sean. He looked up and down the riverbank, but saw no sign of the elderly couple.

He busied himself with stringing his line, threading it through the eyes attached to the rod. He then attached the leader line, and the last act was to attach the fly to the leader. The twins followed the instructions.

"Did you boys see how I did that?" He checked their poles. "Good job. Now, let's go fishin'."

Kinden walked a ways up river and Kevin turned down river.

"Whoever catches the first fish gets out of KP duty for the rest of the day," shouted Sean. He waved to the boys' before he tossed in his line.

*This is so cool,* thought Kinden. He didn't really care if he caught any fish. He actually had to admit to himself that he was enjoying being out in nature. Just then, he heard a rustle in the bushes. He turned and saw Annie and Jocko standing on the bank.

"How's fishin'? asked Jocko.

Kinden noticed Jocko had a whole string of fish already. All pan-sized, clean. *No mortal could have caught and cleaned that many fish in such a short time,* thought Kinden. He looked downstream to see how far he was from his dad and his twin. But they were no longer in sight. *I'm not scared of them,* he whispered over and over like a mantra.

"Can I give you a fishin' tip?" asked Jocko.

"Sure. That would be cool." Kinden reeled in his line. "You and Annie catch fish in a hurry."

Jocko didn't answer. Instead, he cast his line downstream from where he stood on the bank.

"Always look for a swirl in the water, near a boulder, where the shade is," he said. "If a big fish is looking for shade, he'll go on that side of the boulder to get out of the swirling part of the water. Now…you want to try?"

Kinden did as instructed. He cast his line, but nothing happened. He reeled it back in. That was when Jocko noticed the fly Kinden had attached.

"Oh! I forgot to tell you what kind of bait to use. If it is hot, like today, fly hooks don't work too good. Flies work better when the skeeters are out and the fish are jumpin' for them. Like maybe in a couple more hours."

Jocko smiled at Kinden. "Here is what you need. You need a worm." He reached into his pocket and pulled out a small tin can full of mud, He dug around in the mud until he found a wiggling worm. "Here, put that on your hook."

Kinden took off the fly and stuck it into his cap like Jocko did. He opened his fly box and found a bare hook that he tied on to the leader. Then he reached for the worm. He squirmed a bit, but he put the wiggly worm on the hook.

With a deep breath, Kinden cast his line again, back into that shaded spot by the boulder.

Snap! His line went tight. The rod bent into an arc. Then the line started whistling as it shot out over the water, faster then Kinden could stop it.

"I got one, Jocko. I got me a fish!"

"You do for sure. Don't lose him! He's a big one and a fighter. Tighten the drag. Pull back! Careful…keep that line tight. He's a real fighter. Start reeling him in."

Jocko jumped off the bank into the shallow edge of the water. He reached into his hip pocket and pulled out a small net and scooped up Kinden's fish.

"He's all yours, Kinden. Good catch," said Jocko. "You listen well, young man. I'm proud of you."

Kinden found a large rock and killed the fish. He turned around to show off the fish, but found that Jocko and Annie had disappeared, and he was alone.

"Dad…Kevin! I caught a fish…where are you guys anyway?"

"Mosquitoes be gone!" shouted Kevin into the ether. A cloud of smoke followed him. "I'm the most handsomest here. The smoke found me first and, you know, smoke follows beauty." Kevin danced around the bonfire.

"You guys ever made a S'more? It's a marshmallow and chocolate and a graham cracker," asked Kinden.

"Laws yes. We love the challenge it takes to roast that marshmallow just right. Usually mine bursts into flames and falls into the fire pit, but tonight? I feel lucky. I'm goin' to make me a masterpiece."

Annie reached for the marshmallows and took out two, one she handed over to Jocko. He, in turn, had picked up two pre-pointed willow sticks that the boys had brought to the fire pit earlier in the evening. They poked their marshmallows onto their sticks, and gingerly leaned toward the fire flame.

"The secret is to not put the marshmallow into the flame," offered Kinden. He very carefully kept his stick to the edges of the flame, letting the heat turn the candy into a golden, roasted, caramelized mass.

"Quick! Hand me a cracker and a chocolate square." He mashed the concoction together and smelled it.

"Ummmm…." He popped the whole treat into his mouth and crunched down on it. "Ow! That's hot!" He fanned his face while everyone else laughed as he jumped around, flapping his hands.

Everyone, in turn, made his or her sweet delight, and the evening progressed in sacred time. Sean had served his hearty coffee to the guests, and conversation was light and fun. It just seemed right that the elderly couple should be sitting at their fire, enjoying the treats, laughing happily, and slapping at an occasional mosquito.

Had they looked out beyond the fire's flames, they would have seen glowing yellow eyes as a mountain lion, walking through the meadow in search of some dinner, stopped to stare at the circle of friends.

Jocko heard the big cat and worried a bit, knowing it was headed the same direction that he and Annie would be walking back to their cabin.

"Annie? Ready to go? The moon is full tonight to guide us back across the way." He stood up...reached for her hand, and yawned.

"Let's say goodnight, now. Mornin' comes mighty early in these parts."

He paused for a moment and looked right at Sean. *What is it about this fellow? I must be slippin' that I can't place him.*

As he and Annie faded into the darkness, Sean and the twins heard music. Jocko was singing an Irish ditty in a clear, tenor voice. *"Is minic a lean maidin bhrónach oíche shúgach. - 'Tis many a sad morning followed a merry night."*

# ~ 8 ~

▼

# BEDTIME

Jocko sang loudly and clomped around in the grasses to make noise. When they had all been seated about the campfire and the flames were high, a wild mountain lion would never approach unless sick. But, away from that flame, the scene would change, and the big cat was in control of his territory.

"Isn't this a lovely night? Look...look at that huge, moon?" Annie walked a brisk pace, sensing something in Jocko's behavior. Their cabin was close, and the walk ended without incident. Jocko did not fear any harm for himself, but he was concerned for the campers.

He wished he had mentioned the cat to Sean; to alert them to take flashlights to the outhouse, for example, and not leave the cooler outside with food stored in it. He didn't want to set up a fear in the twins. Well, he'd make sure he brought it up in the morning. Now it was bedtime.

Jocko paused at the door and looked back the way they had come. He saw that the fire still burned low in the fire pit. Silhouetted bodies, like dark shadows, were running around in the yard.

*They are probably pouring water from the pump in the yard onto the fire.*

"Jocko? Is somethin' wrong? Botherin' you? Come inside."

"In a minute, dear. I'm looking at the stars shining so bright tonight."

He looked back at where the cabin claimed the land, and a peace filled him when he saw the cabin light extinguish.

"Coming Annie." Jocko let the door slam behind him.

"Kinden told me his dad is a firefighter in the summer time, and a math teacher at the high school in Helena in the winter months. He said Sean worked the Sawmill and the Rock Creek Fires last summer, and that's how he found out about this place," said Annie.

Jocko frowned.

"That must be where I saw him, last summer, when they were working around our cabin." He took off his shirt and sat on the edge of the bed.

"Does it bother you to have strangers in and out of our place, Annie?"

Annie reached for his hand. "Come to bed you old fool. We can't control any of that any more, but we can have fun with the strangers who do come to rent our place. And, look how nice the Forest Service people fixed the old place up." Annie sighed. "We'll just have to get used to it, Jocko."

Then, as if remembering something unusual, Annie chuckled. "I love having the company around. We could be a welcoming committee sitting inside the locked cabin when they opened the door."

Jocko picked up her merry mood and laughed with her. "Meeting Fisher Jack and Auntie Annie would certainly give them something to talk about when they hightailed it out of there."

Annie pulled down the bed cover. She reached for her long, flannel nightgown hanging on the hook by the bedroom door. She unwrapped her head turban. Black curly hair fell about her shoulders. She ran her fingers through the tight curls, as was her nightly routine. Always keeping her head covered, Annie pulled on her knitted nightcap.

"Here this car comes into our yard from Helena, just a few hours ride. Why, when we were living here, it would take days to go to Helena for a visit." Annie sighed again.

"Years ago, I dreamed of spending a little time in Helena with the colored community. To sing in the choir inside St. James Free Methodist Episcopalian Church...I wonder if that is still a church? Probably not any more...and, to 'take tea' with Mrs. James Crumb after the services, well, it always stayed just outside my reach." Annie put her hands palms up in her lap.

"The ladies gathered weekly for parties and dinners and quilting. Oh! I got invited, but I never could be gone from that old cabin for a trip to Helena, even in the summer time." She sighed. "For me there was just no way. There was no one to relieve me from my duties with Judge Durfee's ailing uncle." She stood up and stretched. "Then you came along, and my life changed altogether."

Jocko sat very still on the edge of the bed. He'd removed his shoes and noticed a hole starting in his right sock.

"I'll always be grateful to you for looking for me when my horse turned up in your yard. I would have drowned in the creek if you hadn't come looking."

Jocko walked around to Annie and gave her a warm hug.

"You cured me of typhoid using those herbs you always have stashed by the kitchen door." He looked at himself in the mirror hanging on the wall by the dresser. "No way was I going to let you get away." He very tenderly massaged her shoulder.

"We made a good couple back then, didn't we?" He didn't wait for her to answer. "Hey! We make a good couple right now, don't we?"

"The best, Jocko…then and now…the best."

A mosquito buzzed around inside the dark bedroom. Jocko listened to what sounded to him like a buzz saw. Finally, he could take it no longer. He noticed Annie was asleep, or maybe pretending to be. He jumped out of bed, hoping to find the insect that was keeping him awake. Finally, unsuccessful in his attempt to get the mosquito, Jocko fell back on to his side of the bed and covered his head with the sheet. Morning light would be just around the crest of the mountain, and Jocko had a busy day planned for the boys. It was time to take them exploring in the old barn.

# ~ 9 ~

▼

# JOCKO STORIES

The boys felt at home in Annie and Jocko's bunkhouse. Annie doted on them lovingly, and Sean knew she would keep them occupied while he went fishing.

The fancy rod and reel was light and balanced in Sean's hand. It was a joy for him to cast into the swirling waters. The huge boulders catching the water sent it cascading over and around the rocks. He sensed the stream was talking to him this morning. All was right in Sean's world today.

He saw smoke coming from Annie's chimney when he glanced back towards the buildings. He could barely hear his sons' laughter as it carried on the morning breeze across the meadow to his ears. A smile covered his face as he thought about how the vacation was going.

It was a good decision to take off this summer and spend time with the twins.

*I wonder what Judy is doing at home*, he thought. She had a long list of projects, one being to finish a quilt that she had started about a year ago. To watch her cut the material into little squares, not bigger than three inches, was a lesson in patience…hers, not his. *She'll probably get that quilt finished before we get home.*

Sean's line stretched tight and then started to spin out of control. "I've got a big one," he shouted. He raced along the bank, playing with the fish for a few minutes. "This is breakfast. Umm-umm good."

- - - - - - -

"Bacon's ready. How many eggs for you mighty campers?" Annie held up a spatula, waiting for the chorus to answer.

"I'll have two eggs, some bacon, a slice of toast and jam," said Jocko.

"Can I have one egg and one piece of bacon and some toast, too?" asked Kevin. Kinden just finished washing his hands and sat down at the wooden table.

"The same for me, Annie. Thank you," said Kinden.

"Yeah. Thank you," said Kevin and Jocko in unison. Jocko drank from his coffee cup and set it down with a bang.

"Now I am going to tell you about my huntin' and trappin' and fishin' days," he said.

Annie stepped away from the stove with two plates, filled to order for the boys. Jocko looked at Annie with pride in his eyes, and when she set his plate in front of him, he took her hand in his.

"My, my. This must be some story comin' on," said Annie. She lingered for a moment with her other hand on Jocko's shoulder. Then she sat down with a hot cup of coffee.

"You know, boys, it wasn't always like this here on Rock Creek. Why, Annie was a livin' out here all alone, with a horse and wagon to get her to town, when I came on the scene. She needed a man around, and I came at the right time."

Annie slapped him on the arm.

"What did you do for me?"

The boys laughed and ate their hearty breakfast, forgetting their dad all together. When Sean walked up on the porch, waving his eight-inch trout, it was Annie who went to the screen door to let him in.

"Laws, Sean. Give me that fish. Pour yourself a cup of coffee while I fry it up for you. Umm-umm. Nothin' better than a fresh fish right out of that river."

"Dad. You're just in time. Jocko's going to tell us about when he was a trapper and hunter," said Kevin.

Sean swung his leg over the chair seat, and sat down. He looked about the bunkhouse. *They lack for nothing*, he thought. *I wonder…*

The fish sizzled in the bacon grease and Sean turned his head back toward Jocko to listen to the story he was spinning.

*Look at their faces,* he thought. *This is just perfect. They will remember this vacation when they are both old and stressed out like their old man.*

Jocko had the Irishman's story telling knack, and the boys, entranced by his words, were still and attentive.

"I was just a few years older than you two when I came west," spoke Jocko. "I enlisted into the War of Inconvenience, you boys ever hear the Civil War called that? I was a Union soldier out of New Jersey." He didn't wait for an answer.

"The Civil War ended with me being with Gen. William Tecumseh S. Sherman, and we marched through Georgia to the sea." Jocko shook his head sadly. "That was not a good time for our country, boys. I hope they teach you in school about that war."

The boys squirmed, not really understanding what Jocko meant about the war that happened over one hundred-forty-five years ago, and that he was a soldier then.

"I didn't want to return to New Jersey so I headed out west to sign up with him to fight Injuns. That's what I did. I fought Injuns. Now they were some brave and strong fighting men." Kinden and Kevin were holding their breath, not daring to even move or speak.

"We marched all over the southwest, boys. We looked for Sitting Bull, and Chief Joseph, and Apaches, and Navajos, and Blackfeet and Sioux. We found 'em, too." The memories were forming in Jokko's head. It had been a while since he had a captive audience. He took another swig of coffee. Annie put the cooked fish on a plate, and set it in front of Sean.

"Aahh, Jocko. Did you really fight Indians?" asked Kevin. "What kind of a gun did you have?" Kinden nudged Kevin to shut up.

Jocko looked around the table. He wondered how much to reveal.

"Oh! I am getting away from telling you about being a trapper and fisherman here in Granite County." Jocko changed the tone of his voice, as he began again with another facet of his youth, exposing his past to these modern 21$^{st}$ century boys.

Sean savored every bite of the freshly caught and fried fish.

## ~ 10 ~

▼

# TRIP FOR SUPPLIES

Sean left camp very early to make the run into Philipsburg for more supplies. He had talked it over with the boys at dinnertime the night before. They had immediately started a list of foods they couldn't live without. It was only Wednesday, and already they were craving snacks. They needed more chocolate bars and graham crackers, and marshmallows. (Apparently, the Girl Scouts long ago knew their campfire confection would be a favorite on the menu at every outdoors fire pit.) S'mores and a campfire were a must, for their-soon-to-come last night in camp.

"Be sure to bring tons of ice for the coolers, Dad, and some pop, too." The July sun grew hot earlier every day, and bottled water was a must on the list. The three of them were drinking more water than originally planned.

The boys had made it quite clear they did not want to go with him. They had things to explore on the property: things like old hay rakes and buildings. The twins were asleep when he drove out of the yard. He'd be gone several hours. According to his plan, by leaving this early, he'd be back by late afternoon.

He drove through the pole gate and walked back to shut it. It was then that he took notice of the historical marker. *When I get back, I must take time to read that sign,* he thought.

Sean was a man with two missions this beautiful morning. Mission one was to shop first for groceries, then get the ice and more bottled water. He had packed the biggest cooler into the Subaru in order to keep the ice cold.

Mission two was to find someone to visit with about the papers the boys had found in a leather pouch inside a coffee tin while searching through the old barn.

*Once a firefighter always a firefighter,* thought Sean, as he noted it had been a great place to keep important papers from danger of fire. Cabins with fireplaces, and/or wood cook stoves often went up in flames. *Huh! I always thought papers were kept behind mirrors and picture frames.*

Sean enjoyed the special quiet that came over him as he retraced the road back to town from the cabin in the woods. It gave him time to think about the progress he was making with the twins, the fun they were having being "just us men," as Kevin called it.

An added bonus to the trip was the odd couple, Annie and Jocko. They were dressed like they belonged to another century, but the clothes were not tattered or faded. *I'll have to take a walk over to their cabin and have a talk with them.*

They were staying in a rustic bunkhouse. They just seemed to pop up at the right time, whether to join them around the fire or for a lively discussion about fishing: catching fish, eating fish, fish recipes, fish stories, and more. *The man knows an awful lot about fishin',* thought Sean. He reminded Sean of someone from his past, but it eluded him. *I guess he reminds me of Great-Grandpa James,* he thought. *When I get back home, I'll look him up in the old family album.*

The older couple was good company for all three of them, and Sean found it a good mix of generations. The boys' grandparents lived in another state, and the boys really didn't know much about them. *I have to work on that and bring our families together more often,* thought Sean.

*I am making progress in bonding with Kinden…he's happy and busy. I liked it when I saw Kevin playing baseball in the yard, things like that. They both are enjoying fishing every day, and cooking and eating their catch, too. I like some of Annie's recipes for cookin' fish.*

Sean smiled as he drove along. Already he was collecting memories of this trip. How excited Kinden was only a couple of days ago, when he won the contest for catching the first fish. *We're makin' memories…good ones. I wonder how things are going at home. Judy probably misses the boys. I think I'll take time to call her.*

Off in the field stood a beautiful buck deer. His ears were pointed towards the car noise, and his flight instincts had his tail twitching. The sun shining on his hide made the hair look glossy.

*This is going to be a perfect day,* thought Sean, as he relaxed behind the wheel. The open road and the warm sunshine on his arm completed the picture of a contented man. He heard humming and realized it was coming from deep within him.

The turn-off to the road leading into Philipsburg came too soon. He pulled into the convenience store on the edge of the highway, filled up with gasoline, picked up the snack foods and, for good measure, put fresh bananas, apples and oranges in his basket.

"Might as well take advantage of it, mister," said the man behind the counter, as he held out his hand for Sean's credit card. "Pay for it all inside, and pick up the ice on your way out."

Turning on the left blinker, Patrick slowly made his way into the town. He carefully crossed the railroad tracks and took his first real look at the town. The angle of the morning sun cast a golden glow illuminating both sides of the street. Church steeples punctured the blue sky on the left hillside.

Then it came to him. Deja vu. *I remember seeing that same light when I was just a kid, coming over to Rock Creek with Grandpa James. Dad and I had to sit on overturned paint cans in the back of that old black Ford panel truck.* He chuckled out loud. "Sure couldn't do that now."

It was from his grandpa that he'd developed the love for fishing, and it was a sport that had stayed with him. Now he was enjoying it once again with his own boys. *I've got to call Dad when I get back to Helena and have a long visit with him. He'll get a kick out of it. Maybe I'll talk him into coming in August, and we'll all come camping here. I'll check out the B & B in town and give Judy and Mom a vacation, too. They'd love to check out all these quaint shops.*

The freshly painted stone, brick, and wood buildings, mostly built in the 1800s, lined the extra-wide main street. He drove past a candy store, a couple of antique shops, a general mercantile, and a jewelry store. The town was coming alive right before his eyes, as storefront doors were blocked open to the street, and OPEN signs were flipped over. At the café, he watched old-timers sitting on stools at the counter.

I thought this town was an old mining community, a ghost town. But I guess the people livin' here forgot that… or…maybe I am drivin' into a twilight zone?

Sean continued his way up through the town. *The boys would get a kick out of seeing this place. When we are packed up, I'll stop in town so the boys can walk around a bit before we head back for home.* Then he spotted the ice cream parlor sign and clicked on his right blinker. Slowing to a crawl, he found a parking space. Already the street was crowded with tourists, even at this early time of day. Sean looked at his watch, and was surprised at the time. It was mid-morning. Cars, with license plates from all over the United States and Canada, lined the sidewalks, front-end in, making more room for parking.

Sean looked in the window of the ice cream parlor and suddenly remembered he'd skipped breakfast. He was growling hungry. The bell tinkled a friendly sound when he opened the screen door, and he went inside. A smiling waitress gave him a friendly wave.

"Hi. Can I help you? Sit wherever you'd like, and I'll be right over, sir."

Sean spotted an old ice cream store, wire-backed, round-seated chair, and sat down. His eyes darted all about the long, narrow room filled with antiques and photos of early day Philipsburg and the miners. One photo, showing four men and a dog, reminded him of someone, but he didn't know whom. *Hhmm…I wonder if Jocko ever had his picture taken.* An old bank vault stood guard on the wall right behind him. The soda fountain looked ancient, and a huge mirror ran the whole length of that back wall. He looked up to the menu board hanging high on the back wall.

When the waitress approached him, he already knew what to order. "I'll take coffee, black, and your lunch special, if its not too early." He smiled at the woman. "I'll be needing some of that vanilla with crushed strawberries ice cream, too."

When the waitress returned with her freshly made pot of coffee, Sean asked her for information. He needed directions to a museum.

"Yes, sir. We have a great museum just down the street and around the corner. Turn left and walk up a ways 'til you see a large building on the right side of the street. You can't miss it."

Sean finished his generous portion of soup and sandwich. But he still wanted that vanilla crushed strawberry ice cream. He changed his order from a dish to a scoop in a cone.

"Enjoy," said the waitress. "Oh! Across the street from the museum is the Playhouse. Are you staying in town? Be sure to take in a performance, if you are. There are matinees on the weekends, too."

"Well, not this trip. I am camping and fishing on Rock Creek, and I came in for more supplies. My boys are eating me out of everything, including pork and beans." But Sean liked the idea of coming in to town on their last day.

Sean enjoyed every bite of the oversized scoop of ice cream.

"Is this ice cream made here?'

"Some flavors are," she said in passing.

"That vanilla and strawberries combination you chose is a recipe from a woman who lived in the area in the late 1800s."

The waitress moved all about the room pouring coffee, cleaning tabletops, always busy and smiling.

"You should work for the Chamber of Commerce, as a tourist information person or something." He paid the bill and tossed a tip on the table.

"See ya'."

He pushed open the screen door, again hearing the tinkling bell. He got his bearings on the street, and walked to the end of the block.

*I'll get some ice cream before I leave town to take back to the boys.* He had already picked up the ice for the camp coolers, and he would put the ice cream inside the cooler. But he didn't want to purchase it now. He still had part two of his mission to investigate.

"My name is David Letford. Are you visiting us for a few days? If so, may I recommend a stay at Quigley's Country B & B?" He smiled and Sean instantly felt at ease. "I heard you say you were from over Helena way? We have a writer from Helena who comes to visit us."

"Well, it's a great place to visit. However, the reason I am here in town, and not on the river fishing, is about this pouch and its contents. I'm hoping you might give me some information about the people whose names are on the document." Sean spread out the paper. It was faded, having been written in pencil, but still legible and readable.

"I'd like to take a look-see at that paper."

Sean pushed it across the counter top.

"My, my. Where did you ever find this?'"

"It's a long story. I am a firefighter, and I was here fighting the Sawmill/Rock Creek/Hog Back Mountain Fire. I helped save the Morgan-Case cabin when we wrapped it in foil. Last winter, I heard it was up for rent this summer, so I applied for a week's stay. My twin boys and I are enjoying every minute of the greatest fishing stream in Montana."

He smiled and held out his hands, indicating his fish catches were at least a foot long every time.

"My sons were exploring an old barn, and they found this pouch inside a coffee can. When we opened it, I felt it might be something significant to the cabin, and the people who lived there."

He looked back and forth at the faces of the two people. He noticed they were excited to read this antique find.

"Sir, I believe you have found the original, hand-written draft of the will Annie Morgan wrote out. Look! It's not signed…just like the legend states," said David.

He pointed to the end of the will, and there was no signature. But the names 'Agnes Annie Morgan' and 'Joseph Case' had been spelled out in the body of the document.

"The story goes around here that Annie came to town to have the will properly drawn up by a local judge. She planned to return to sign it her next trip into town." A frown crossed his forehead. "Unfortunately, for both her, and her common-law husband, Joseph Case, the document was never signed. Annie died before they returned to town."

David laid the paper down on the counter top.

"She wrote it out in long-hand to make sure it said exactly what she wanted it to say. See here? She wanted the homestead to go to Joseph Case."

"Old Joseph Case had to work at improving the homestead for another five years, re-filing on the land in order to have it legally in his name. He did it; followed the letter of the law even though he had lived there and had worked that land for over thirty-five years."

"That's a sad story," said Sean. "Did they get it straightened out?"

David interrupted. "Why don't we go get some iced tea or coffee? It's my coffee break time." He started walking toward the main entrance, and then stopped.

"Didn't you say you had two boys with you? Where are they?

"I left them at the cabin. They had plans, and didn't want to come into town for supplies. They are old enough, and savvy enough, to be careful if left alone for a few hours. There is another older couple in the bunkhouse just across the edge of the field from where we are, and they seem to want to be grandparents to my boys."

He saw David stiffen.

"Um…there's just an empty bunkhouse on that property." He walked back to the counter. "You said you have seen this couple?"

"Yeah. Sure. Why?"

"What do they look like?"

"The woman is black. She wears a turban or a scarf wrapped around her head most of the time, and the man seems to be of Irish descent and has a white, cropped beard. He loves to talk fishing.

David rocked on his boot heels, as Sean felt panic rise up in his gut.

"What's going on? You tell me…who are those two?"

"Now, don't get upset, there fellow. I think Annie Morgan and Joseph Case's spirits are taking a vacation, right along with you and your boys."

David stopped and scratched at his right ear, then continued.

"Look at you. You're as white as a sheet. That ghost story is over one hundred years old. Lots of folks claim they see that odd couple near the cabin. But they are always friendly."

Sean left the pouch and paper on the counter, ran out the entrance, and back to his parked SUV.

My boys! Oh, dear God, let them be fine. Guardian angels watch over them. Keep them safe from any harm from those ghosts. I believe the story. I've seen them. *Sean repeated this prayer mantra all the way back to the Morgan-Case cabin.*

He pulled in front of the unopened gate, jumped out and flung it as far open as he could. He ran into the yard, leaving the vehicle by the gate.

"Kinden…Kevin! Where are you? Show yourselves right now."

# ~ 12 ~

▼

# STRAWBERRY ICE CREAM

Sean started running towards the old bunkhouse.

"Kevin…Kinden? Boys? Come here! Now!" The blood coursing through his veins had gone right to Sean's brain, and a blinding light flashed behind his eyes. His flight or fight adrenalin tightened his spine. The muscles in his arms bulged.

"Kevin…Kinden…Answer me."

The rustic bunkhouse door burst open, and the boys, plus Annie and Jocko, came out onto the wood porch.

"Hey Dad. What's all the yellin' for?" Kinden motioned for Sean to join them.

"Come on in, Dad. We found an old bucket with a crank on the lid, and Annie told us it was an ice cream maker. Did you bring back ice? We, uh, kind of used up the ice we did have in the coolers."

Sean ran to his boys. He grabbed the twins, each by an arm, and pushed them protectively behind him. They struggled to get free.

"What's goin' on, Dad? Let go." The twins squirmed, trying to free themselves, but Sean stood his ground. He confronted Annie and Jocko.

"I know who you two are. Don't deny anything. We'll be out of here in a few minutes. Boys, get to the cabin, and start packing up."

"Dad. No! We know who they are, too. We didn't tell you, because we knew you'd make us go home if you found out. It's okay. We aren't afraid of them. We want to stay. You will, too, when you find out about them."

Jocko stepped off the porch, and walked toward Sean.

"I'm sorry, Sean. We were just having a little bit of spirit fun. We don't normally show ourselves, but our spirits will always be on this homestead. Your boys are great. And, we wanted to share this place with you. I've been having me a grand old time giving the boys fishing lessons, for one thing."

Jocko turned to Annie.

"We're going for a walk, Annie. Be back in a while." He turned Sean back towards the meadow. "Let's go back up by that gate you left open, and we'll have us a talk."

Jocko walked right alongside of Sean. "Your boys are fine and safe with Annie. Why, she'd never hurt a flea."

Hesitantly, Sean walked back the way he had come. His heart still thumped, but it had stopped pounding in his chest. He continued to turn around to keep check on the boys. They were still standing where he had left them.

"I went to the museum in Philipsburg with that old leather pouch…to show them the papers of Annie's handwritten will. Why didn't you say something yesterday?"

"For one thing, we didn't know you'd be taking off for town, and we did plan to explain things to you. We talked today with the boys, and they are both "cool" with who we are."

Jocko had a destination in mind, and he continued to walk as he talked. "Your boys are very bright. Especially Kinden. He thinks we'd make a great TV series, whatever that would be. But, we'd never have the energy for anything so bold. I doubt anybody would be able to see us either. Going to the Opera House in Philipsburg to scare the beejeezus out of the newcomer performers each season, is about all we can handle these days."

As the two walked, Sean eased up a bit. Jocko motioned for Sean to walk over and read the sign located on the opposite side of the fence.

"Your boys read this sign the very first morning. When Kinden saw my clothes he suspected something was not quite right. In fact, he and Kevin are pretty brave younguns. They told Annie and me 'they weren't afraid of no ghosts,' and Kinden told me I looked like I belonged in a museum."

He looked down to the ground. "It was the laced-to-the-knees fishing boots that gave me away." He swung his right foot back and forth. "These old boots are still the most comfortable pair I've ever worn."

With that Sean laughed out loud. He continued to read the sign, and when the words "Fisher Jack" jumped right out at him, he took a step back.

"Fisher Jack? Are you the same Fisher Jack that fished with my Great-Grampa James?" Sean put his hand to his forehead.

"This is incredible. Ever since you got here I felt I knew you from somewhere." Fisher Jack was lost in memory.

Sean sat down in the grass.

"You saved my Grampa James' life. Do you remember that?"

Jocko thought a moment. "Great-Grampa James Patricks, and his son, James. He'd be your Grandpa James. Yes...yes, I do remember that fishing trip.

"Did I save his life? Well. It depends on who is telling the story, I guess."

"My Grampa James still talks about that fishing trip with his dad. My Grampa James almost drowned here in Rock Creek when he was about eight years old. He's in his 80's now and still talks about that fishing trip."

Jocko interrupted Sean.

"He was fishing on the bank, and he got too close to the edge, and it caved in on him. I pulled him out before he came to a row of huge boulders. He would have died hitting those huge rocks."

The whole scene was flashing before Jocko's eyes.

"I remember hanging on to his shirt."

Jocko smiled at the memory.

Sean looked at Jocko.

"My Dad, whose name is James, by the way, isn't the fisherman that Great-Grampa James was. He had a job that kept him away from the fishing streams. But you know what? He and I have had a few good fishing trips on the streams and lakes near Helena. He taught me to love nature, and to appreciate the river and to catch dinner. The same things I am trying to instill in my twins with this trip. James, my dad, and Ellen, my mom, are now retired, and live in Arizona in the wintertime, and Helena for the summer months.

Jocko smiled and walked toward the front of the cabin. He sat on the huge tree stump that easily held two or more people.

"Annie and I sit on this stump and eavesdrop on people who rent this cabin. Some we like, most we don't, 'cause they want to bring the city stuff with them, all them electric gadgets."

Jocko looked out toward the river. "We very seldom use the energy it takes to show ourselves, as it does tire us and shortens our time here."

Sean eased himself down on the stump.

"Tell me more, Fisher Jack. I want to hear about you and Annie."

Jocko fidgeted a bit, not knowing where to start or how much to reveal in this conversation. It had already been full of enlightenment for both men.

"You know, I told Annie the first time you drove in the yard that you looked familiar to me, like someone I knew." Jocko chuckled. "Wait till I tell her about this. She'll remember it, too."

Jocko put his hand over his heart. "James Patricks' great-great-grandsons are fishing Rock Creek with me. My, my. This is truly a wonderful moment for me, boy." He shut his eyes and paused only for a moment.

"Maybe your dad could come over sometime, too. You are welcome here any time."

Jocko let his eyes drift toward the bunkhouse.

"You don't know it, but Annie fished *me* out of Rock Creek. That's how we got together. I was delirious with typhoid fever, and I fell off my horse into the creek. She heard the horse coming into the yard and ran to find me. She did, too, face down in that cold water, half dead. She pulled me out and dragged me into her cabin. She nursed me for weeks with her herbs and soups."

Sean sat very still.

"Well, after a few weeks of doctoring, I was up and getting strength back. I didn't have any money to pay her, so I worked it off by building these old barns, and that chicken coop over there. See that fence...that pole fence over to the right? Well, I built that back in 1880, and that fence is still standing." He pointed toward the stream.

"I guess I was a good enough hired hand, 'cause we been together ever since." He smiled. "I knew I was in love with Annie the first time I opened my eyes and saw her looking so worried down at me as I slept in her bed. I asked her to marry me." Jocko smiled as he continued the memory.

"You know what she said? She said, "I ain't hookin' up with no white man. Never. I's a freed woman, and I got papers to prove it. No siree, no man'll never own me, never again. You's welcome to stay on here as long as you want, Fisher Jack, and sleep in my bed, and we'll take good care of each other.""

"Well, that was her answer to my proposal. It was good enough for me."

Sean saw a smile curve on Jocko's lips.

"Can you imagine our surprise when we went to town one day with a load of vegetables out of her huge garden? We met up with a lawyer. He asked us if we knew we could never legally marry in Montana Territory. No sir. No wedding bells would be ringing out our black and white names."

"Well, that just cracked up Annie right there. She belly-laughed me all the way back home." Jocko grew pensive. "We did all right by each other. I still love her with all my heart. I came out west looking for adventure, and what I saw was the elephant." He opened his hands and spread out his arms enveloping the whole area with his embrace.

"We worked this homestead for over thirty-five years, together. After she died in the spring of 1914, I stayed on until 1927 or so." Jocko wiped a tear from his eyes. "That was the hardest time of my life, losing my girl."

Sean felt calm now. He put his hands over his head and stretched. He started to walk toward the SUV still parked by the open gate.

"I need some help getting that ice cooler out of the Subaru, Jocko. You able to lift one end?"

He brought the vehicle up to the yard and parked it. The two men quickly unloaded the groceries and put the huge cooler inside the kitchen.  Jocko started walking across the meadow.

"I'm sorry you had to find us out the way you did, but I'm a bit relieved and glad you know. Now, we can enjoy the rest of your vacation with no secrets, or worries about letting something slip."

"In the morning, let's go fishing. But right now Annie's got that ice cream waiting, so let's go to the cabin and eat it right up." He turned to Sean.

"She made the best ice cream recipes over 100 years ago. Some of those recipes are still being made at the ice cream parlor in Philipsburg. One of the town favorites is vanilla-crushed strawberry. Why we raised the strawberries right over there in that patch." He pointed a little ways off to the left of the porch.

"There are still a few of the original plants surviving all these years. The birds pick at them every day, but we managed to find enough this morning to make ice cream. We were a bit worried you wouldn't have enough ice, and Annie didn't want to snap her fingers in front of the boys."

Jocko laughed at his joke. Sean wondered if it really *was* a joke.

Annie handed him a spoon and a bowl. She held the big dish full of ice cream out to him.

"Fill up the empty one to your heart's content."

"Go ahead, Dad. It ain't goin' to kill you," shouted Kevin. He and Kinden were holding their own bowls filled with a mound of the delicious desert.

"I expect an explanation from you two," said Sean to the boys. "Right after I eat this bowl of ice cream."

With the first bite, he was convinced the ice cream maker at the ice cream parlor in town had used Annie's recipe.

"Did you ever work in town, Annie? At the ice cream parlor, maybe?"

Annie smiled her wide, friendly smile.

"Why do you ask?"

Stump in Front Yard of Cabin

## ~ 13 ~

▼

# SKUNK TRAP

Annie heard the twins long before she saw them chasing each other across the hay meadow.

"Jocko, come look-see. The boys are headed our way and it looks like trouble's fast on their tails."

"Annie! Jocko!" called out Kevin. "Are you guys up? Are you home? We need you."

Kevin was in the lead. A gunnysack he'd picked up in the old barn was bouncing along behind him as he ran toward the old couple's bunkhouse.

Jocko opened the screen door and stepped out onto the porch.

"Whoa there, boys. What're you up to?"

Kinden fell down to his knees in the yard, trying to catch his breath. He took a deep drink of air and tried to speak, but nothing came back out.

"Kevin? Tell me, what's got you two so riled up?"

"Jocko. We're in big trouble," said Kevin. "Last night Kinden and I made a sort of a trap, to see if we could catch us a rabbit." He put his hands out in front of him, palms side up. "We planned to let it go today. Honest."

"Well, tell me more." Jocko stood with his legs apart, knees locked, and arms folded across his chest. He looked stern, disapproving of what the boys had done.

By now, Annie had joined the group as they talked outside in the fresh mountain air.

"Jocko…let the boys tell us their story."

"We just wanted to trap something, like you've been telling us you did."

Kinden kind of smiled at her as if to say, "thank you," and he looked to his brother.

"We caught something in our trap, all right. But, we don't know what to do now. We caught a skunk. He is big and mean, and has a horrible smell all over the place. We don't know what to do."

Annie covered her mouth so as not to let on she was chuckling. Jocko turned to look at her, in order to buy a little time, before he answered the boys.

"Hmm. You do have a problem. What were you going to do with the sack?"

"We were going to cover the cage with it and open the door and let the rabbit out. But when we got there and saw it wasn't a rabbit…. well, here we are."

"Where's your dad?"

"Dad's out on the river fishin', and we thought you could help us better anyhow." Kinden and Kevin shared a look that told it all. "We'd rather not have him know."

"I was just going to have breakfast, but this is more important than eating. Wouldn't you say so, Annie?"

Jocko walked to the side of the house, and found a long pole that had a hook on one end, fashioned out of metal.

"See this here pole? I used it years ago, when I was trappin' animals for meat, for the miners in Granite County. That was how I kept Annie and me in money…was my huntin' and fishin'."

"Can you tell us the story later, Jocko?" asked Kinden. "We're kind of worried about that skunk."

Jocko and Annie joined the twins as they started back across the hay meadow.

Annie looked over toward her garden spot from years ago, and sighed. *I'll have to check and see if there are any apples ready yet. A good apple pie later on today would be a fun project for these two to make to keep them out of trouble.*

Jocko smelled the skunk, and Annie put her handkerchief over her nose and mouth. "Oh! That's the worst smell in all of nature," she cried.

"Boys! Pay attention now. Your idea of the sack is a good one. I want you, Kevin, to toss it over the cage. Do it right 'cause you won't get a second chance to toss it."

Kevin carefully walked closer to the end of the cage, only to have the skunk turn his backside toward him. He stopped and looked back at Jocko.

"Careful, son!" Jocko warned. "You don't want to get hit with a blast of perfume."

Kinden thought time had stood still and everything was in slow motion. He watched his brother lift his arm and give a yell at the same time he tossed the sack. He watched the sack sail across the span in an arc. Kerplop! The sack hit its mark.

"Good toss, Kevin." Jocko looked back at Annie. "You won't have to scrub Kevin down with lye soap, Annie…and I won't have to dig a hole to bury his clothes."

Kinden's jaw dropped as he pictured Kevin standing naked in a tub of water, in front of the cabin, getting the horrible smell out of his skin.

"Now, I'll try to hook the drop latch, and see if I can slide that cage door back up." Jocko studied the gate. "You did a mighty fine job of makin' this here crate out of sticks, I have to admit. You could have caught a mountain lion in this thing."

All the while Jocko was talking softly, he was sizing up the situation.

He took the long pole with the metal hook on the end and slowly, very slowly, walked closer to the covered cage. The skunk could not see him, but knew the human was getting close.

Jocko fiddled around a bit, until he felt the metal connect with a twig. He gave an upward pull from his strong wrists, but nothing budged. Kevin and Kinden stayed back by Annie.

Again, Jocko tried to get the metal under the main twig on the cage door. It had been set to drop straight down when an animal stepped inside the cage, sniffing out the lettuce the boys had put into the far end. This time Jocko had a firmer hold. The door started to slide back up and the skunk scurried toward the cage entrance.

"Just a bit more…and Mr. Skunk, you are on your way."

The skunk pushed against the gate and scooted underneath, free at last. With his tail showing off the white and black fur as it waved back and forth in the air, the skunk sauntered off into the tall grass, headed for the river and safety.

"You boys got off easy this time. You could have picked up a fox in that trap, too. This area used to be called Fox Farm, and there are lots of foxes still in these here parts." Jocko was leaning on his pole.

"Why did they raise fox?" asked Kinden, always the questioner.

"Because foolish women liked to put them around their necks."

Kinden walked next to Kevin, who had picked up the trap to take to the cabin. He asked Kevin if he knew what Jocko meant. Surely women didn't keep a fox as a pet? This called for some further investigation. But then the light bulb went on over Kinden's head.

"Oh! Oh! Women *wore* the *fur* around their neck back in the olden days, and they had that little fox head, with those beady eyes staring at them." He tried to catch up to Jocko to ask him more about foxes, but Jocko stayed ahead of him. He didn't want to talk about fox fur for stylish New York City fashions on an empty stomach.

"Come on, Annie. Let's go get us some breakfast. You boy's hungry? Or do you want to wait for your dad to bring in his catch of the day?

# ~ 14 ~

▼

# APPLE PIE

While Jocko entertained Sean and the boys with stories over their early-morning breakfast, Annie slipped through the bunkhouse door. She headed straight for the apple trees. Even from afar, she could see a few bright red apples ready for the picking. Earlier that morning, even before the boys arrived all worried about their makeshift trap, Annie had been thinking about checking the apples to see if they were ripe enough for eating.

*Isn't that just somethin' to see? Those spindly apple trees I planted over 100 years ago are still producin' the best apples in this county.* Annie smiled. *Looks to me like I have enough to make a fresh apple pie this mornin'.*

Annie scrunched up her long, white apron and tied a knot in the end, making a sort of catchall out of the material. Then she started picking apples.

*I have to take a bite, just like Eve did in the Bible.* She giggled. She polished the sphere on her sleeve first and then bit into the delicious, organic apple. No sprays had ever touched her trees, and the birds preferred to pick higher up in the branches.

"UUUMMM! Good!" Annie finished the apple in about 5 bites and then continued picking enough to make two pies overflowing with nature's bounty.

Jocko was cleaning up the kitchen. Sean and the boys were nowhere in sight when Annie returned to the bunkhouse. She found a large bowl for the apples, and she set it on the round wood table. Annie untied the knot in her apron.

"How does a nice fresh apple pie sound to you?"

Jocko turned to the silverware drawer and pulled out a large fork. He held it up in front of Annie.

"I'll be ready when that pie is."

"Oh, no, you don't. The boys are going to help me make these pies. They need something to keep them out of trouble this morning."

Annie scurried about the kitchen, looking in cupboards for supplies to make the pie. "Iffen I have to conjure up any of the ingredients, I want to do that now, before I call the boys to come and help."

Luckily, it was not necessary for Annie to work her magic, as she had brown sugar, cloves, cinnamon, butter, cornstarch, and one lemon (to squeeze the juice over the cut up apples). She set out flour and eggs. In another cupboard she found a couple of old, dented pie tins and a cookie sheet.

"Now go find those boys and tell them I have a project to work on."

Annie grabbed up two paring knives and the bowl of apples, went out into the morning sun. She put the apples on the top of an old cable-wire barrel that she used for an outside table. "The boys can sit out here on these tree stump stools and peel away."

But Jocko didn't hear her. He had already gone boy hunting.

- - - - - - -

"You pick it up." Kevin sat cross-legged on his cot.

"No. It's your mess. You pick it up." Kinden was standing in the door way to their bedroom. Sean, staying clear of their fight, was outside splitting wood.

"Hello, again, Jocko. The boys are arguing as usual about their stuff." Sean shook his head. "You'd think it would be so simple to just pick it up, wouldn't you?"

Jocko smiled. He noticed the shirts and pants hanging on the railing, airing out. A hint of skunk hung in the air. Neither man made comment of it.

"Annie wants the boys to come help her with a cookin' project. She says that will keep them occupied for a couple of hours."

He shouted into the cabin. "Boys! Annie wants you right now. Come on, hop to it."

The men heard feet shuffling, as the boys raced to the cabin screen door. "What's it she wants us to do?" asked Kevin. Kinden stood behind him, waiting for Jocko to tell them the plan.

"Just scoot yourself on over to the cabin and find out. I've got work to do with Sean." He turned to Sean.

"It is good to see you are splittin' wood. Annie is goin' to need a lot of wood to fire up the stove and get the oven hot enough to bake apple pies. I'll trade you a slice of that apple pie for an armload of split wood." He leaned over and motioned to Sean to fill his arms with the split pieces of wood, all about a foot long.

"This is just right for her stove." Jocko turned and started walking back across the meadow with his arms loaded. Sean heard the familiar Irish tune as Jocko whistled his way home.

- - - - - - -

"Annie, we came to help. Whatcha doin?" asked Kevin. Then he spotted the bowl full of ripe, red apples on the tabletop. "Do we get to peel apples?"

Annie smiled. "Grab a knife and get started."

It wasn't long until the boys had enough apples peeled, cored and sliced to fill two pie tins. Annie squirted the lemon juice over the apples so they would not turn brown too fast.

"Now, boys. Let's go inside. We have the pie crust to make next."

Annie led the way inside to the kitchen table where she had her rolling pin, pie tins and ingredients to make the dough.

"Kevin you take this side, and Kinden you take that side of the table. We need crust bottoms for two pies." She paused. "Ever made a pie before?"

The boys looked at her as if she had asked them whether they had gone to the moon.

"Heck, Annie. You know we haven't." Kevin rubbed his arm with his other hand, while Kinden scratched at the side of his nose.

"Okay then. Here we go." It wasn't long before the boys, following Annie's instructions, were up to their elbows in flour. They were rolling, turning and fumbling with the pliant dough. Kevin lifted his flattened-out mound of dough just as Annie scooted the pie tin under his hands. He carefully folded the dough into the bottom of the pie tin just as Annie had instructed.

"Well, would you look at that? Mom will never believe it."

"Dad won't either," spoke up Kinden. "Annie, help! Here comes my pancake, too." Kinden dropped his circle into the other tin just in time.

"Well, how's the pie makers? I've brought wood for the stove." Jocko dropped the load into the woodbin alongside the stove and opened the firebox door. With flour clear up to their elbows, the twins went over to watch Jocko, as he built a fire in the old Majestic stove. "We have to get this a-goin' for Annie's pies."

"Aw. Jocko. These are our pies. Annie just told us how to do it." Kinden and Kevin gave each other a little shove.

"Boys, get back here. We have the fillin' to make, and the tops to roll yet."

The boys scurried back to their chairs, leaving a trail of flour across the cabin floor. Annie rolled her eyes. "You two got to clean up the mess, you know."

"Kinden get the sugar bowl, and Kevin get the cinnamon," instructed Annie.

Happily, the boys measured out the ingredients, mixing, pouring, and tasting with their fingers as they coated the sliced apples. Then they dumped apple slices as evenly as they could into the two pie tins.

"Okay. Now we make tops, right?" asked Kinden.

"You know what to do, so have at it," said Annie. She walked to the stove and checked the heat gage on the oven door. The temperature was slowly rising as the wood burned evenly.

"I want to make a design on my pie top, like a smiley face," said Kevin.

"Let's put a sun ray picture on mine," said Kinden.

Annie picked up a fork and showed the boys how to crimp the pie dough that was hanging over the top.

"We have to seal the edge to keep the juices inside the pie, don't we?" Then she let them finish that job. Next, she took a sharp knife and started to cut off the excess pie dough. "Here, you two. Finish up the job." She handed the knife to Kevin. He finished his pie and handed the knife to Kinden. Both boys looked extremely proud of their efforts.

"One last step," said Annie as she brushed the top of the pie with whipped egg whites. She then sprinkled a bit of sugar onto the top.

"Bring the pies to me, and we will put them on this large cookie sheet," said Annie. "We don't want the juices that should break through to spill out and make a terrible mess inside the oven."

Annie had second thoughts, and she held up her hand.

"Just a second boys. We have to test the heat in the oven before we open the door, and slide in the pies."

Annie gathered the scraps of pie dough. After rolling it out, she took a drinking glass and turned it drinking edge down to cut into the pie dough. This made a circle about the size of an orange. She looked at Kinden, who was leaning up against the counter top with one foot on the floor and the other foot stuck in the chair support.

"Kinden, hand me the sugar, please." She sprinkled sugar on the circle tops.

Annie then pointed to the remaining pie dough, and the boys took the hint. They made circles, too, filling a flat tin sheet with their soon-to-be cookies.

"Will you look at that? We can't waste one speck of that good, sweet dough, now, can we?" Annie smiled.

"This is the way to test the heat of your oven, by putting in a couple of circles to see how long it takes to brown the dough."

She felt the heat when Kevin lowered the oven door. Kinden shoved the tray, filled with the dough, onto the wire shelf. In just a few minutes, Annie peeked inside the oven. She reached for a thick hot pad. It looked like she had made it years ago, from an old cotton dress she had cut into strips and weaved, like a very tight basket-weave pattern. Kevin held a pancake turner, waiting for the order to scoop off the cookies onto a cooling rack. His mouth watered as he thought about eating one of these cookies.

"It smells like Thanksgiving time in here."

"Yeah," said Kinden. The heat from the oven was warming up the bunkhouse really cozy. "It's a good thing it is still early morning, 'cause that stove sure is goin' to heat up this place."

Annie carefully lifted out the cookie sheet and with the pancake turner, slid the cookies onto a plate. She closed the oven door, and checked the gauge once more before putting in both pies, one at a time.

"There. We are done. Hey! Guys, we made a pie." They high -fived each other in turn, and Annie grabbed their hands.

Jocko walked in about then. He dropped to his knees. He had his fork all ready to dig in to the pie.

"Please, Missus. Can I have some pie?" he teased.

"Oh, no you don't," scolded Annie. "You get out of our kitchen. We'll call you when it's ready to eat." They all laughed, as Jocko scooted out of the kitchen on his knees.

The boys helped Annie clean up the spilled flour, and then they swept the floor. Kinden brought in more wood that Jocko had left stacked on the porch. The delicious aroma filled the room, but Annie did not open the door, not once, even to peek at how the pies were baking.

"Thank you, Annie. That was fun. We didn't know making a pie took so much time and work. I bet this is going to be the best pie ever made." Kevin washed the utensils they had used for the pie-making project, and Kinden dried.

"We'll get the ladder out of the old barn, and pick apples if you want us to. We can help you make applesauce."

Annie smiled. "We'll check the trees tomorrow, and see how ripe they are. We can pick them every day as long as you are here."

She saw a frown on the twins' faces. "Oh, I said something wrong?"

"Annie. We want to stay here all summer with you and Jocko."

"Now that is a wrinkle." Annie looked squarely at the boys. "Your mom and dad would miss you." She hurried over to the oven and called the boys to join her.

"Let's check the pies." They made a space for Annie to open the oven door. "UUUMMM!!! Look at that. Just right timing on that crust. Hand me a fork, and I'll poke an apple and see if it is soft enough."

Annie poked into one of the pies. The apples were soft, and the top gleamed a golden brown. Using her potholders once more, Annie pulled the pies from the oven.

"Where to set them?" She looked around the room, and decided to put them on the outside porch table.

Kevin took off running for their cabin. "Don't cut it. Wait! I'm getting my camera."

Sean heard the commotion, and put down the book he was reading in the shade of one of the huge pine trees. Actually, he was so relaxed, the book had been lying across his stomach. He realized he had been sleeping in the hammock.

Kevin was in and out of the cabin, screen door banging, and camera in tow. He raced back to Annie's porch and the pie. Sean jumped up, and ran over to the bunkhouse to see what the commotion was all about.

"I want pictures of this pie. I wish I had thought to bring the camera with me earlier while we were making it, too." He looked up at Annie.

"Can we do this again, so I can prove to Mom we made it?" Annie nodded and laughed.

## ~ 15 ~

▼

# EATING THE PIE

The boys, acting like there was nothing to do, slumped their elbows on the wood spool table. Annie gave them the long awaited cookie and scooted them off the porch.

"Be off with you two. Go catch me some fish for lunch."

It was only eleven o'clock in the morning, and the boys had already emptied a handmade trap that had held a captured-by-mistake skunk. With Annie's help, they had made cookies, and two apple pies. Cleaning up the kitchen seemed like hard work, but now even that job was behind them.

"Yeah! Let's go fishing." Kinden looked around for Jocko, and spotted him down by the river. "We can fish with Jocko."

The boys scampered back to their cabin where the fishing gear was stashed alongside the outer wall. "I'll beat you to the river," shouted Kinden who was not to be outdone by his brother.

"Well, will you look at that," said Sean, as he rocked on the porch. He was drinking a bottle of water. "My boys are changing right in front of me. I think I'll catch up and go fishing with them."

Earlier in the morning Sean had gone fishing, but now he got up, stretched his spine, and walked toward his gear leaning up against the porch railing. He loved the sport. He enjoyed being out all alone in the cool morning air, watching the world wake up around him, the early sun spreading warmth throughout the valley.

The river was happily rolling along, calling, singing out to the boys to try their skills at catching a creel full of trout for Annie to fix for lunch. Sean smiled at their good luck to have Annie and Jocko interested in playing with his twins.

It wasn't but sixty minutes later that all four fishermen had three fish each, varying in sizes (but none smaller than six inches) cleaned, and ready for Annie's hot skillet, already coated with bacon grease. She'd dip the fish in whipped eggs, coating them in cornmeal, before carefully laying them into the hot skillet.

Annie had been peeling potatoes to make hash browns, and she had also picked a few fresh peas in her vegetable garden.

A pump-handle well gushed with good, clean water. Years ago, Jocko had rigged up a pipe that she hooked over the spout when she wanted water in the garden. The long pipe saved her miles of walking steps every day. A large trough, located in the garden area, allowed Annie to dip her watering can into the trough and then sprinkled the rows. The wild animals liked to drink from this trough and Annie and Jocko enjoyed watching them sneak into the yard for a drink.

Early every morning, one could find Annie tying up vines, and checking for tomatoes. Her below ground vegetables always did better, since the season was so short, but she didn't care. Pesky rabbits determined to chew their way into the garden during the night. Jocko, in years past, had strung a chicken wire fence to keep out the deer, but it was a lesson in futility.

Annie thought a moment as she looked over the garden spread. *Why, back when I was a young, freed woman, livin' out here all alone, it was nuthin' for me to feed campers all the fish they caught, and make them coffee, apple pies, strawberry shortcake, and hand-churned ice cream. I let folks pitch a tent or two and stable their horses. All for a mere 50 cents a day.*

Annie stood up and shielded her eyes against the sun's rays. *I like it when Jocko and I can show ourselves. I know it tires us, but we love this valley, and this place so much that our spirits will never leave here. The people in Philipsburg still talk about us. We lived through some mighty hard winters, the two of us did. I'll have to get Jocko to tell some more stories about the "good ole' days.*

At exactly high noon, the four fishermen wandered back into camp. Content with the vacation, and each day's adventure, the quartet made its way to Annie and Jocko's bunkhouse.

"Annie! Annie! We've got fish. You have four hungry mouths to feed, and we're starving for that apple pie for desert," shouted out Jocko.

"Can we have permission to come inside?" He stood at the edge of the bunkhouse door, and stuck the willow tree switch with the fish strung on it inside the partially opened screen door. Annie jerked the switch right out of his hands.

Jocko turned to Sean and winked. "That there is Army talk. It drives Annie crazy when I tease her like that." He smiled a knowing smile. "Actually, she likes it, just doesn't want to admit it, even after all these years of being together."

Sean waited for Annie to answer, and sure enough, just as Jocko predicted, she said, "Permission granted for three of you only. You chose which three."

"Well, that wasn't what I wanted to hear," said Jocko. "Looks like one of you twins is goin' to have to wait on the porch." With that news, Jocko and Sean entered the kitchen.

The twins stood, dumbfounded, not knowing what to do next. But Kinden, quick to respond, turned to his brother and said, "Annie? Since we are twins we count as one." And the two boys scampered inside to join in the fun of cooking lunch.

Annie, Sean and Jocko looked at each other at the same time, and burst into laughter. "Come. You've earned your lunch, for sure," said Annie. She motioned the boys to chairs at the table.

They ate lunch in silence, knowing what lay ahead. Finally Annie stood up.

"Now is the time to cut the pie," said Annie. She walked to the porch and brought in both pies, never worrying that flies would bother their masterpieces.

"Which of you two boys can figure out how to cut this apple pie in five equal pieces?" The twins looked at the pie very carefully, and Kinden grabbed the sharp knife. "Can I take one piece out of the other pie?"

"NO!" answered the resounding chorus.

"Heck! That's an easy math question." But still, he studied for another couple of minutes, until Jocko grabbed the hand that held the knife. "Cut the pie, NOW!" Kinden divided the pie into five perfect pieces.

Each took their fair share of the pie, and savored every bite.

"Annie, how long you been bakin' pies and cookin'?" asked Kevin.

"Well, now, that is a bit of a story that goes wa-a-a-y back, boys. When I was just a little girl, I worked alongside other slaves on the most beautiful plantation in the whole of the South. I was an inside slave, so I learned to do genteel things, like sewin', and to cook delicious meals for the master. The mistress of the house taught me to read and write." Annie set down her fork and looked around the table at the faces staring back at her.

"Then as I grew stronger and older, I worked in the huge vegetable garden, hoein' and weedin' and carryin' buckets of water. One of my jobs was to graft apple trees and plant bushes. It soon was clear that I had a knack for herbs and could make my own medicines. When a slave was injured in the field, the overseer would send for me to come and make plasters, or stop the bleedin' with my potions."

Sean looked at his sons' faces. They were staring straight at Annie, as if seeing her for the first time. Obviously, they had not put the dates together earlier in the week.

Now, with the story she was telling, it dawned on them that the heart of this woman had beat over 140 years ago, strong and pure. Annie had been alive and endured the Civil War. Now she was a spirit and they were eating and talking with her and Jocko. How could they wrap their minds around this?

The twins had studied a smattering about the "Civil War," or the "War Between the States." They had even learned their lines in a play in the 6<sup>th</sup> grade at school. The play depicted a civil war hero, Brigadier General Thomas Francis Meagher, who became the first acting territorial governor of Montana Territory.

Placing Annie and Jocko in that time frame was more than they could handle.

First Kinden stood up and asked to be excused, and Kevin followed on his heels. They ran to the river's edge and stopped at a little dugout they had found earlier in the week.

"Man, that was spooky."

"Yeah. We knew they were spirits…but this…" Kinden waved his hands in circles over his head. What do we know about real ghosts?"

# ~ 16 ~

▼

# ANNIE'S CONCERN
## FOR THE BOYS

"What did I do? What did I say?"

Annie looked bewildered as she searched Jocko's face for an answer.

"Why did the boys run away like that?"

"Ah! Annie. You just gave out more information than the twins could handle. Let Sean talk to them now and see what comes of it." Jocko sighed.

"Could it be I frightened them with my story? Oh! No! That just cannot be." Annie lifted both her hands and covered her face, trying hard to hold back tears.

"Why…laws, Jocko, you know I'd never…." Her voice trailed off.

Jocko walked across the scrubbed, plank floor and took the quaking woman into his long, strong arms to give her a warm, protective hug.

"Give it time, Annie. We'll have to see what Sean does." Jocko paused in thought. "He might pack up, or he might take the boys fishing. Either way, we'll know soon enough."

He patted Annie on her shoulders, and backed away from her, only to sit

at the kitchen table.  He had to think what to say and do next.

"I had a good talk with Sean the day he came back from Philipsburg. He was all upset about thinking the boys were in harm's way.  After I told him how we can show ourselves on occasion and for a short time. He was good with it then."

He reached up into the cupboard for a clean coffee mug.

"How about making me a fresh pot of coffee?"

Being needed brought Annie back to her senses. She bustled over to the stove, looked into the coffee pot and, using a corner of her apron front, brought the pot to Jocko.

"Here you go. There's still plenty in the pot. I got work to do besides waiting on you hand and foot." Annie filled his cup, and Jocko smiled up at her. He knew she would weather this storm of passing between being a spirit, and dealing with humans.

"Annie. You and I will forever be a part of this here homestead. We just got involved with those rascal boys and forgot who we are. But you'll see. They are smart, and they'll be back for more. We'll just have to be careful how we word things from here on out." He had crossed his fingers when he made this last statement, and...Oh! How he hoped it was true.

"Let's plan a bonfire tonight, and I'll tell a story about you during the Civil War, and how you met up with General Custer." He laughed. "It'll seem more like a history lesson, than a life story lesson, coming from me."

"You old coot. You always did know what to do to bring me around. No wonder I let you stay with me all these years." Annie gave his cheek a pat.

"Now go do something else, will you? I want some peace in my cabin again."

Jocko stood up and stretched.

"These past summer days certainly have been full, haven't they? I guess I'll go check the garden patch for you and water the rows."

To be honest, Jocko was happy to escape the bunkhouse. He stood in the shady side, and peered over the wire fence at the vegetable garden. He liked watering the patch and worked hard at the weeding. He had strung a wire fence, necessary to keep the deer out of the space that was growing, among other things, peas, potatoes, onions and carrots, all eventually ending up in one of Annie's delicious soups.

Jocko turned and faced the river. He watched Sean and the boys walk up from the riverbank to sit on the huge stump near the cabin. The conversation was intense, he could tell, by the way they were all looking at each other.

*Please, for Annie's sake, let's find a happy meeting ground.* Jocko thought.

*At least they didn't go inside to pack up.* Jocko was pleased with that thought. It meant they were trying to wrap their heads around the fact that they were actually seeing and talking with spirits.

*I think it's time I mosey on over and join them. I have something to say about all of this that will help us.* Jocko walked out of the garden, and shut the makeshift gate behind him. He wondered what kind of a greeting he'd be hearing.

- - - - - - -

Sean walked slowly towards the oversized stump. He needed time. Things were spiraling out of control, and he didn't know how to stop it. For some time now, he had known about Annie and Jocko. Since the day he had driven to Philipsburg and had gone into the museum to show the curator the leather pouch, he had known.

*I should have told the boys after I talked with Jocko, but I thought it could be kept a fun game between the ghosts and the twins.* Now he had to try and explain what was happening in this twilight zone they were all caught in. *When we were eating ice cream, they seemed squared away with the whole idea of ghosts and stuff.*

"Boys, let's sit on the stump for a minute. I want to talk to you about what Annie said back in the cabin."

The boys had been walking ahead of their dad. They scrambled up on top of the stump, and scooted over so all three of them could sit. Sean chose to sit between the two of them. They all had their backs toward the cabin so they could look out into the meadow and watch the river.

The river held a certain fascination as it rolled swiftly and continuously, as if time itself would not change.

Sean spoke in very soft tones. "Boys" he said. "We need to talk."

"Dad, what's going on?" The boys looked at Sean for answers, and he hoped he got it right.

"Straight out, boys. Annie and Jocko are spirits of the people who lived here over one hundred years ago. They like to stay in this beautiful homesteaded spot, because it was their home way back then." He paused and looked at the twins' faces.

"From what I can figure out, if they like the campers, they will show themselves for a while." Again, Sean paused to see if there was a reaction to what he was telling them.

"Dad, the very first day when we read the sign by the gate fence, we knew WHO they were, but we didn't think of it as anything but a game. Now, after listening to Annie and Jocko talk this morning, it scared the beejeezus out of both of us." Kinden waved his hands in circles in the air.

"Geez, dad. We are just kids, you know?"

Sean hid a smile by wiping his face with the back of his hand. "This is what you two were keeping from me this past week? I knew there was something." Sean stood up and stretched his back swaying from side to side.

"Okay. Now we know what we are up against, what do we do about it? Are you afraid? Do you want to pack up and go home? Or…do you want to go fishing?"

The boys were startled by their dad's questions. They looked at each other with a questioning face, and a shrug.

"Kevin? What do you think?" asked Kinden.

"This has been a great week, and we only have today left. We will be packing up to leave in the morning." Said Kevin.

"Annie and Jocko have been so much fun. I'm not afraid of them." Kinden hopped off the stump.

"We have wood for another campfire tonight and stuff."

Kevin and Kinden and Sean did a high-five.

"Lets go fishing!"

# ~ 17 ~

▼

# SEAN'S BACKGROUND

The walk through the woods on the south side of Annie's homestead gave Sean time to stretch after his lazy morning. He still savored the memory of the piece of apple pie made by his twin boys the day before. He whispered a special "thank you" prayer for this time he was having with the boys.

When he first came up with the idea of taking this vacation, he met with opposition from both Kinden and Kevin. They wanted to spend summer time with their friends playing ball, hanging out, and doing boy things. But Sean had wanted more. He could see they were growing up without him. Oh, they were still a family, and he was still "Dad." But Sean was searching for something deeper and more meaningful for all of them. He wanted to create memories with, and for, the boys.

He had lately found himself watching his dad growing older. Sean wished he could, somehow, turn back the clock to those gone-forever years.

His dad worked hard for the family, and Sean and his siblings appreciated and respected him for the commitment he had fulfilled, day-in-day-out, as a mail carrier in Helena. Sunday was go-to-church day at their house. Occasionally, during the summer especially, his dad would announce in his own flourish and style that a great weekend outing at Park Lake was scheduled, rain or shine.

His mother would send them off with huge, cardboard boxes full of supplies, for a weekend of eating. Pans, and utensils to cook eggs, bacon and pancakes on Sunday morning. She teased them with hotdogs for their Saturday night supper (just in case they didn't catch any fish), jugs of lemon-aid and water, snacks and fruit.

The old Buick station wagon bulged with gear, including fishing poles, volleyball nets, card games and kids. Sean smiled, as he remembered the way they must have looked to passers-by. They traveled up the graveled road with kids hanging out the rolled-down windows and the old dog's shaggy head braving the wind in his nose, eyes and ears.

Sean wanted that type of family memories for his boys to pass on when they became adults. He shook his head to clear it.

- - - - - - -

When the fires of 1910 destroyed thousands of acres in Idaho, Washington and Montana, including many in Glacier National Park, the federal government enacted laws setting money aside to create an agency. Over the years, the University of Montana in Missoula, added the program to its curriculum. Hundreds of young men joined up, learning to spot fires in fire towers built by the CCC corps.

These men were stationed in national parks throughout the United States where the need for summer firefighters had grown to major proportions. Now, in 2009, this agency consisted of a year-round operation involving thousands of federal and state employees. Fire equipment, fire knowledge and safety, and public relations, grew with the need of the Forest Service. Hot Shot crews, developed on the Indian reservations, soon held the reputation for bravery above and beyond their call to duty. The files quickly filled with heroic rescue operations each fire season, along with credits given to these fiercely proud men.

The National Forest Service, once started out of necessity, now reminded Sean of a giant octopus, with tentacles wrapping around separate divisions of the organization itself.

*I wonder if Jocko remembers fires that came through here,* thought Sean, who finally had accepted the fact that Jocko and Annie were spirits. *I must make it a point to talk to him about any involvement he might have had as a young man living out here in this remote area of Hog Back Mountain.*

Sean walked until he came to a burned-out area. He watched the dead timber swaying, and he recognized the danger he'd be in if the wind picked up, toppling burned-out trees. He could hear them crashing deeper into the forest.

A small herd of mule deer trotted out, unconcerned about his presence, as they ate the green shoots emerging out of the blackened dirt. Off to the right, and down in the valley floor, he recognized a farmhouse his crew had wrapped last summer in the intense Sawmill fire.

The heavy, thick aluminum foil rolls and duct tape surrounded many of the more vulnerable houses in the direct path of the fire. Even the roofs were protected from flying torch-like branches. It took hard work, and many hours to complete a wrap, but it always saved the building.

Everything seemed back to normal. The outbuildings looked sturdy. He could see a man on a ladder, painting the house the same color it had always been. The big barn had a new coat of red. Sean's heart swelled with pride at what his men had been able to save. Everything the farmer owned was tied up in the land. His hayfields were again full of alfalfa. The little feeder stream meandered past the front yard where a couple of dogs were chasing each other.

The only remaining evidence of the fire was char-blackened tree trunks, swaying in clumps. There were hundreds of shade trees, newly planted in a shelterbelt, along the south side of the property. From where Sean stood, they looked like Russian Olive and Quaking Aspen trees, two varieties that would grow quickly.

With another winter, this family directly below his perch, might forget some of the horrors of that summer's fire. Maybe this summer they would not be forced to breathe acrid smoke, as uncontrolled tears streaked their faces. Hopefully, no one would have to be evacuated from their property.

Many were angry, striking out at the very people who were trying to move them out of the dangerous path of the fire. Every wind change brought hidden concerns for the firemen and, as the days slowly wore on into months, frustration mounted to fevered levels. Daily reports, issued to land owners, kept them informed as to their property's status and where the fire had passed through. Many were spared great losses thanks to crews working 24/7. Sean held his men in high esteem.

The families, up and down the Rock Creek road would, this summer, be able to ease their tension and fears. Finally, they would enjoy a night's rest after a good day's work in their renewed fields. The ash in the soil had been good for the present crop, and the grasses, newly sprung up in April, held a deeper green than had been seen for many years. Obviously, a good hay crop showed promise of a second cutting. The first cutting dotted the fields in heavy, rolled-up, bailed grass.

Sean remembered that first emergency call. This fire had begun at the first of June and didn't stop until the rains from Mother Nature put it out in late September.

Not only was it a long fire season; it was a demanding one as well. The men spent long hours patrolling and spotting. They slept in sleeping bags in tents, and their camp looked like an Army settlement.

The cooks worked 24/7 preparing nutritional, high-calorie meals, starting the next meal before the last one was even consumed. The men worked hard in between meals, and it was the cooks who kept them happy with good quality food. Coffee pots held steaming brew at all hours and, as soon as one was emptied, it was refilled for the next crew coming in off the line.

As Sean stared off down into the valley floor, he wondered about the decision he had made last fall. Did he mean it when he had promised himself he was going to spend summers away from the firefighting crews, and instead, become involved with his family?

He wrestled with this question all that winter and into the spring, as he continued to teach during the school year. He had tenure at the local high school, and his salary matched his tenure. He had planned to work for the Forest Service as a fire fighter until the twins were out of college. But, in reality, his age and aching bones had begun to bother him, along with the heat and smoke and all the problems associated with living in a firefighter's camp.

- - - - - - -

*He makes more noise than a pack of dogs running through the woods after a deer*, thought Jocko. He watched Sean walking the trail directly below him. Jocko would meet up with him near Fisher Peak.

*I spent most all my time huntin' up in these here hills. Whatever I could shoot or catch in a trap went into the stew pots, providing meat for the miners working in Granite County mines.* It kept Jocko busy, from sunrise to sunset, hunting for game.

Fishing came easy to Jocko, and he enjoyed casting his silk line into Rock Creek. *I wonder how many thousands of fish I've pulled out o' that there creek?* He smoked fish by filleting them and laying them on wire racks in a handmade smoker. He used an old metal barrel, stoking firewood into the side opening for many hours, until he had a full box. Then he'd take the fish to the mines for sale. The miners always were happy to see him arrive in camp.

Jocko skinned all the animals and did the butchering. He dried the hides by skinning off the fats and sinew that remained on the inside, and then he hung the hides on the fence to dry. He tanned each skin, using the brains from the animal as a tanning agent. One Grizzly bear hide hung in the barn.

In his mind's eye, Jocko could still see that huge, humpbacked, spooned-in -nose, grizzly bear that once had towered up in front of him on the trail leading to the hidden lake up on Fisher Peak. The horses had gone nuts.

*That ol' hoss gave me quite a ride. I remember thinkin' I should shoot that cayuse. But I never did. That horse could pack hundreds of pounds without problems to his hoofs. It took several shots to bring down that old bear, but it was either him or me.* Jocko chuckled.

Jocko kept that bear hide for years. He didn't want to sell it, and he was careful not to brag about it in the mining camps.

Jocko picked up his pace, determined to catch up with Sean on the trail. Sean was meandering, obviously deep in thoughts of his own.

*I was surprised at how well he took the news about Annie and me being ghosts.*

# ~ 18 ~

▼

# TIME TO PACK UP

Sean left the cabin so quietly even the proverbial mouse didn't wake up. He walked across the kitchen floor in stocking-clad feet. He had left his boots near the kitchen door when he'd taken them off last night. He hoped they were dry enough to put them on now, as he didn't want to hunt for his shoes. The boots were damp from the grasses he walked through while fishing late into the evening the night before.

*I don't want the boys to wake up just yet. I want some time alone to take a walk up on the hillside and think about this vacation with the twins.*

Little did he know that the boys were wide-awake, lying very still in their beds, waiting for their dad to slip out the door.

"He's gone. Let's us get gone, too." Kinden's bare feet hit the floor. He slipped into his jeans, and then pulled a sweatshirt over his head, almost at the same time. "Come on, Kevin. Get up."

Kevin rolled over and looked out the window. Traces of sunlight greeted him as he stretched his arms over his head.

"I'm up. Okay! I said I'm up. Don't throw your pillow over here."

Kevin hurried to pull on his clothes. He, and his brother, had a mission this morning, and time was of the essence.

It was their last morning at the Morgan-Case Homestead cabin. Neither of the boys wanted to leave.

They grabbed some hamburger buns that they found in a plastic bag on the kitchen counter, and chewed on them, as they hunted for their boots. Finally dressed, they raced out the door hoping their dad was far away from the cabin by now. They were sure he wasn't going fishing. None of them would want to have to clean fish this morning. It was time to get packed up to return to Helena.

The boys had noticed that their dad had come back with an empty creel after fishing for a couple of hours late last night.

"Dad, you probably didn't even have a hook on your line," joked Kinden.

Sean had laughed. "You are so right, Kinden. It was just too nice to come inside. No mosquitoes for some reason." He was a contented man, but he also knew the time was near to start packing for their morning departure. He planned to drive into Philipsburg to give the boys a good look at the town. They could stop at the ice cream store for lunch, and taste the homemade strawberry ice cream one more time.

"Better get to sleep boys. Morning is going to come too early for us." Sean sat on the edge of his bed, pulled off his jeans and heavy sweatshirt, laid back on the mattress, thankful it was a good box spring, fairly new. *I must remember to thank the Forest Service for this great bed,* he thought. He was asleep before the boys.

- - - - - - -

From high up on the side of the mountain Sean watched the sun rise. The sky looked bright blue. Golden swirls were inside fluffy white clouds. It was so bright where the sun centered, that he was forced to squint his eyes.

As he turned away from the awesome sight, disgusted with himself that he had not grabbed the digital camera left on the kitchen table, something caught his eye. It was a couple of early morning deer, making their way on a well-worn path, headed for an open meadow to graze.

But something else stopped him. There were the twins heading for the river. *Now, what are they up to this morning?* Sean stood very still.

- - - - - - -

"Come on, Kinden. Keep a sharp eye. We've got to find it."

Kinden, as usual, walked about 15 steps ahead of his brother. He had taken off his shoes and socks, and left them on the bank before wading into the water.  He was at a low point in the water, trying to step on rocks.

"We have to find it."

The boys walked downstream farther than they knew they were allowed to go, but it was something they had to do. Not ready to give up their search, Kinden let out a yell.

"Over here! Hurry!" He pointed to something metal hanging in the middle of a chokecherry bush on Kinden's side of the riverbank. "Look up. High! There! Look in that bunch of really tall bushes."

Kinden scrambled down to the river's edge and tried to see what Kevin could see.

"See it?" He pointed. "There it is! I knew we'd find it if we looked hard and followed the water far enough." Kevin was dancing on his toes; he was so excited.

Kinden wished he had brought his fishing pole to act as a stick to knock the object out of the bushes. He struggled a bit, trying to shake the branches. Finally, the object dropped to the ground, and Kinden gingerly made his way to where it lay. The river had a sharp bend, and the water swirled around rocks, but he was careful. Luckily, the object fell on the bank and not into the cold water.

"I've got it! I'm going back up stream to where I left my shoes and socks. That's where I crossed over. Let's get back to the cabin before Dad finds out."

The twins made their way back, but not before their dad. Sean, when he spotted the boys downriver, had returned to the cabin. He made coffee for himself and sat on the porch. Sean looked over to the right of the cabin, where an abandoned wood stove sat, rusted and falling apart.

*I wonder how many times Annie made coffee on that old wood stove? I am very grateful for the electricity the cabin has today. But it is great that there is a wood stove in the kitchen for cooking*

"Well. Hello, you two. What have you been up to?"

Kinden was clutching something to his side, like he was carrying a football.

"Dad...Look! We've found Jocko's reel. We know it's his. Look!"

Sean stood up and reached for the old reel. He turned it over several times, and then, just as Jocko had described it to him, he saw the initials J.C. scratched inside one of the crossbars. The turn crank was still in place in the metal.

"You have a real find there, boys. What do you plan to do with it?"

The boys looked at each other, surprised by the question.

"A...a...a" sputtered Kinden. "We want to take it home to show our friends that we had a ghost with us."

"Yeah," said Kevin. "They won't believe us if we just tell them about Annie and Jocko."

"Wrong answer, boys." Sean smiled at his sons. "This is one story we will be keeping to ourselves. Of course, we have to tell Mom, but nobody else."

He thought a minute. "I know you boys want that reel for a souvenir, but it isn't ours to take. It belongs here with the cabin and the memories."

Sean walked over to the huge stump. He set the reel on the bare top and walked back inside the cabin.

"Let's get packing," he shouted over his shoulder.

Many trips were needed to load the Outback with all the camp gear that seemed to have multiplied over the past week. Each time the boys walked outside they looked to the stump. The rusty old reel actually took on a glow in the morning sunlight.

"Hey! I wonder where Annie and Jocko are this morning?" mused Kevin. "It would be fun to give Jocko back his lost reel wouldn't it?"

The boys understood why they couldn't take the reel with them to town, but they didn't like leaving it on the stump for just anyone to come by and take. They worried about that, hoping against hope that Jocko and Annie would come by before they left.

They had said their goodbyes last night, when they used up the last of the chocolate bars, marshmallows, and graham crackers, making S'Mores .

"Oh! How I love these tasty morsels," said Annie, as she grabbed for her marshmallow, that was about to drop off of the stick into the fire. It was noticeable to the twins that Annie and Jocko both seemed to be tired out.

"Everything secure?" asked Sean, as he slammed the hatch door shut. "Kevin, get the gate."

Kinden and Kevin both raced to the gate, and Sean drove through.

"Dad! Stop!" yelled Kevin. "Look, Kinden! The reel is gone from the stump. I knew Jocko would come by to be with us until we left."

Patrick jumped out of the Outback and stared. Sure enough, the reel was gone. He saluted back towards the stump. Apparently, Jocko did not have enough energy left to visit one more time with the boys and Sean.

"Come on, boys. Everything is where it is supposed to be."

"Dad? Jocko must have been here all along. I'm glad he has his old reel back." Kinden hung his head.

Sean saw the hesitation in the boys. What a difference from the day they had arrived over a week ago. Neither boy had really wanted to spend this vacation time with their dad at a remote cabin in the woods.

They drove away in silence, lost in their own memories of the past wonderful days. About eleven miles down the road, Patrick thought he saw Annie and Jocko. A hairy, black-and-white dog, lay by Annie's side as they were picnicking where Willow Creek joined into Rock Creek.

Sean didn't stop or mention it to the twins. Philipsburg and lunch were now on the boys' minds. Would the ice cream at Doe Brothers Ice Cream Store taste like Annie's ice cream? Naw!

As if waiting for them, David, the man Sean had met in the museum, was sitting at the counter, drinking coffee. They greeted each other, and Sean offered David his hand to shake.

"Say hello to Mr. Letford, boys."

"Well, so this is the last day of your fishing trip? I kind of thought it would be. I was wondering if you'd follow me up to the cemetery after your lunch? I want to show you the tombstones for Annie Morgan and Joseph Case." He looked at the twins.

"Now, I'm not asking any questions. But, if you did meet up with them in their homestead, it would be good for you to put them back into their resting places. Can you take the time?"

"Yes!" shouted the boys in unison. Sean smiled, as he thought about David's strange statement. "We want to see the cemetery."

While they ate their burgers and fries, David regaled the twins with stories about early-day Philipsburg, but he also tossed in a few stories about his own youth as a cowboy on the Hog Back ranches. For good measure, he filled them in on what life in Alaska in January was like. He would never run out of stories, not David.

Sean followed David's Jeep through the town.

"Dad, look at that sign painted up on top of that old building. It says L. Shodair Green Grocery….something. It's faded out. Could that be the same Shodair Hospital name? Our hospital, where we had our tonsils out?"

"That is something to check out, guys. Let's make a telephone call when we get home. More than likely, Mr. Shodair donated money to the hospital, and they named it after him. That would be my guess."

At the cemetery, David easily found Annie's stone. A white obelisk, it stood strong and proud against the blustery winds, rain, snow, and cold, as a monument to a fine woman. *Mrs. Agnes Morgan, 1914,* greeted them. It was the backside of the stone that caught Sean's eye*: Cooked for General A. Custer. A good neighbor and liked by all her knew her.* A clump of silk daisies had been poked tenaciously into the ground on the backside of the stone.

"Dad, the dates don't add up. Annie was at least ten years older than she told us," said Kevin, always the math student.

David's laugh was a deep, happy laugh. "Why so it is. She probably kept her age a secret from Fisher Jack all those years. He was younger than her."

Had they only looked over a few stones, to where *Joseph Case* had been chipped into the large piece of granite, they would have seen Jocko giving Annie a friendly shove to her shoulder as he, too, laughed.

"Aw, Annie. I knew it all the time. But it didn't matter. I just didn't want to ever leave you after I finally found home." He wiped a tear from his eyes.

"Remember the first time we went to Philipsburg, and on the way home you said, 'Jocko, one lifetime isn't goin' to be long enough?'"

Annie nodded.

"And I said, 'Then we'll just stay here forever?'"

She nodded again.

Annie reached over and took his rough and gnarled hand into hers.

"Come on, you old fool, let's go back to the cabin. It's peace and quiet there.

## ~ Today ~

▼

If you drive the short road up the hillside to the Philipsburg, Montana cemetery, you will find their stones. But you won't find Annie and Jocko there. Many fishermen, over the years, have reported to old-time Philipsburg residents that they thought they had caught glimpses of an old couple while fishing and camping in the meadow.

Who knows?  Maybe, if you get close to the river and listen to the water swirling around the huge rocks, you will hear Annie as she calls out to Jocko.

*"Let's go fishin, Jocko. Come on, Bingo.
The river's callin' us."*

Photo No 8 Rock Creek

# Acknowledgments

Once again it is my privilege to thank my sister, Ellen McKelvey Murphy, Helena, MT, for her photographic and computer skills in putting together this second novel, and for composing the covers, front and back.

Sharron Ensign, Helena, MT, for her computer skills and patience with the author.

Patrick McKelvey, my brother and firefighter, who fought the Sawmill Complex fires of 2007, and to whom this book is dedicated.

Carla Hall, Albuquerque, NM editing skills.

Mari Katherine Hodges, Helena, MT, researcher and librarian.

David Letford, Philipsburg, MT, who introduced me to Annie's story, and supplied me with much needed information about her homestead.

Loraine Bentz Domine, author of *Mettle of Granite County*, whose friendship and knowledge supplied me with much-needed names and places of the area in the 1880's.

Mary Bell, Helena, MT, writer and friend who encouraged me every step of the way to tell Annie's story; to stretch myself with the second part of the book.

Kinden and Kevin, Sean and Judy, Ellen and David are created from friends and family.

Mouser and Bingo are "cool" animals in my life.

Montana State Historical Society, Helena, MT.

Archival staff University of Montana, Missoula, MT.

# Biography

Author Biography:

Lenore McKelvey Puhek
P.O. Box 2006
Helena, MT. 59601
E-Mail: lpuhek@gmail.com

Born and raised in Montana to pioneer stock, my surroundings, landscape, people, home and friendships feed my desire to write.

I am a member of Western Writers of America, The Montana Historical Society, and a charter member (1982) of Writers in the Big Sky. I enjoy being a guest speaker bringing to life special people from Montana's colorful past.

I graduated from Carroll College, Helena, Mt., and hold a B.A. in English/Writing. My writing revolves around Montana historical events, and I have been published in major magazines.

My first novel, *The River's Edge: Thomas Francis Meagher and Elizabeth Townsend Meagher, Their Love Story* was selected by the Montana State Library for an audio book created for the visually impaired and blind.

Past honors include the A.B. Bud Guthrie Scholarship granted for western writing about Montana.

Although I love to travel this earth, Helena, Montana is home.

# Research Sources

## Books:

Allen, Elna Doll, and Arnott, Billie Lou Barnard.: *Montana Homesteaders Reflections & Recipes;* Crow's Printing, Inc., Wallace, Idaho, 1989.

Burt, Olive W.; *Negroes In The Early West*; Julian Messner, NY, Simon & Schuster, Inc., 1969.

Custer, Elizabeth B.; *Boots and Saddles*, Western Frontier Library Vol. 17, Red River Books, University of Oklahoma Press, Norman, Oklahoma (original printing 1861).

Custer, Elizabeth B.; *Tenting on the Plains*, Barnes & Nobles Books, NY 2006 (original printing 1887)

Domine, Loraine M. Bents.; *Mettle of Granite County*, Volume I of 3 volumes; KAIOS Books, Helena, MT., 2008.

Fowler, Arlen L.; *The Black Infantry In the West, 1869-1891*, University of Oklahoma Press, Norman, OK. 1996.

Hafen, LeRoy R., Edited by: *Mountain Men & Fur Traders of*

*the Far West;* University of Nebraska Press, Lincoln, Nebraska, 1965.

Kloss, Jethro; *Back to Eden*, Back to Eden Publishing Co., California 92354, 1939.   (Typhoid, pgs. 442-444)

Litz, Joyce; *The Montana Frontier*, University of New Mexico Press, Albuquerque, NM 2004.

Loewenberg, Bert James and Boyin, Ruth, Edited by; *Black Women In Nineteenth Century American Life;* The Pennsylvania State University Press, University Park, Pennsylvania, 1976.

Lust, John; *The Herb Book*, Beneficial Books, NYC, NY 1974.

Merington, Marguerite, Edited by; *The Custer Story*, Barnes and Noble Books, NYC, 1994.

Moulton, Candy; *Everyday Life in the Wild West, 1840-1900*, Writer's Digest Books, Cincinnatti, Ohio, 1999.

Nacy, Michel J.; *Members of the Regiment, Army Officers Wives on the Western Frontier, 1865-1890*, Greenwood Press, Westport, Connecticut 2000.

Peck, David J., D.O.; *Or Perish in the Attempt, Wilderness Medicine in the Lewis & Clark Expedition*; Far Country Press, Helena, MT., 2002.

Spence, Clark C.; *Territorial Politics and Government in*

*Montana 1864-69;* University of Illinois Press, Chicago, Il. 197 University of Illinois Press, Chicago, Il. 1975.

Steber, Rick; *Women of the West: Tales of the Wild West Vol. 5,* Bonanza Publishing, Prineville, Oregon, 1988

Varhola, Michael J.; *Everyday Life During The Civil War,* Writer's Digest Books, Cincinnatti, Ohio, 1999.

Zimmer, William F., Private; Edited by Greene, Jerome A.; *Frontier Soldier,* Montana Historical Society Press, Helena, MT 1998.

## Web Site Information

Emancipation Proclamation
Gettysburg Address
Morgan-Case Homestead; National Register of Historic Places, United States Department of the Interior, Ntional Park Service, Missoula, Montana.
Barb Wire History; From Open Range to Total Enclosure, Trew, Delbert, 2003
AboutCats.com; So Your Cat is Pregnant.
Wikipedia; Winchester Rifle, History of; from Winchester Repeating Arms Co.
Wikipedia; The Indispensable Civil War Coffee Recipes
Memphis Daily Appeal; Sewing Machines, November-December 1861
An ad for repair work and sales.
Sewing Machines, No. 167., Lienhard, John H.H.
Automobiles 1900 Auburn Automobile.

Automobiles Austin Motor Company
New Jersey's Civil War, History Page, 1861 –1865
Poem; Warshing Clothes, Anonymous

Elk Stew recipe; from the recipe book of Mary Phoebe Payne
Frey, 1880, Maternal Grandmother of Author.

## Photography

All photos are copyrighted and are the property of Ellen
McKelvey Murphy, 2007

LaVergne, TN USA
21 April 2010
179925LV00004B/2/P